Gord

Gordon, Ethel Edison
The Freebody heiress

# The Freebody Heiress

—

Also by Ethel Edison Gordon

# The Freebody
# Heiress

## Ethel Edison Gordon

David McKay Company, Inc.
New York

The Freebody Heiress
COPYRIGHT © 1974 BY Ethel Edison Gordon

LIBRARY OF CONGRESS CATALOG CARD NUMBER: 74-82981
ISBN 0-679-50515-6
MANUFACTURED IN THE UNITED STATES OF AMERICA

# The Freebody Heiress

# 1

*S*exton never looked for the gatehouse, no matter
what anyone thought or said afterward. Neither did he
intend it as a ploy, a deliberate excuse to meet Iris
Freebody. He came upon it quite by chance, on the
Friday before the first week of classes began at the
college where he'd come to teach.

He still didn't have a place to live. He'd been
combing the town without success and that day he
found himself drifting out into the country on a sec-
ondary road, distracted by the beauty of the afternoon. The smoke haze of autumn hung in the air like a
gold mist, the mountains were blue, trees burned in
the sunshine, and a farmer was making a pastoral
whirr, baling hay on his machine.

Sexton had been skirting a long stone wall on his
right for some time. There had to be a house behind it,
but though he thought he glimpsed a chimney, trees
and shrubs made a screen where the wall left off. Here
also were tall iron gates topped by spears, and an "F"

woven into them. Then this must be the Castle, or Adam's Castle, or Old Adam's Castle—terms used by local residents in speaking of the mansion that the Freebodys owned on the outskirts of town. His friend Jeff had told him about the Freebody family, who had given their name to the town, and their land and buildings to found a college which also bore their name. It was Adam Freebody who had built the Castle, his own rendition of castles he'd seen in Europe, and why shouldn't the old boy have built himself a palatial plaything? Adam Freebody had been as rich as the men who'd owned those castles in Europe, maybe richer. Sexton was curious to see how the lords of the manor lived, and he parked his car and walked over to the gates to look through.

The house was tantalizingly hidden. A blacktop drive led away from the gates and then was lost in a thicket of rhododendron and azalea. Practically invisible among them was the gatehouse.

Gatehouse? Gardener's cottage? Old estates still had these small, durable houses built close to the entrance gates, where they could look out on visitors. This one was a ruin. It gaped eyeless out of broken windows, and a door hung half open on one hinge. He climbed up on a rung of the gate to try to see it better. Vines grew luxuriantly over its steep slate roof and clambered undisturbed across the doorway. It was plainly unlived in. The whole effect was rather like the witch's house in *Hansel and Gretel*; he half expected to see some wizened crone appear before him, leaning on a gnarled stick.

2

"What do you want, feller?"

He jumped down off the gate, his heart pumping hard, and grinned at himself for being so startled. On the driveway was planted an old man in a leather jacket worn over a shirt without a tie, a cap on his head.

"I was trying to see the gatehouse over there. Does anybody live in it?"

"Doesn't look like it, does it?"

"Is this the Freebody estate?"

The old man grunted.

"You the caretaker?"

"What I am is my business."

Crusty. "Well then would you happen to know if the people whose estate this is would be interested in a tenant for that gatehouse?"

"You must be a halfwit, feller." The old man cackled. "Why should the family want a tenant? Think they need the money?"

"They don't seem able to find the money to fix the place up. They're letting it fall down."

The old man stopped laughing. "'How they spend their money is their business. You better get along, and keep off those gates, or I'll sic the dogs on you."

He got back into the car, telling himself not to let an old man's surliness get under his skin. Besides, it was getting too dark to see any more. He turned the car around, but all the way back to Jeff and Dodie's house he found he couldn't get the gatehouse out of his mind.

His original thinking with regard to lodgings had

been in terms of some derelict farmhouse he could pick up for a song and then repair himself in his spare time, and it was this plan that had made him head for the country today. He had come out of the army with a little money saved because Frannie, on her salary, hadn't needed any part of it. But there wasn't enough for any respectable property. And after all, he didn't know how long he would stay. Maybe the country wouldn't suit him, and maybe in a year he could forget Frannie enough so that he could go back to New York. But the gatehouse would be a solution. No land to worry about or pay taxes on, and yet he'd have space and privacy, which was what he wanted. The apartment situation in town was hopeless.

Until the end of the Korean War the college had been an exclusive girls' school, its small staff located in whatever old houses in town had turned themselves into flats. Now that the college had tripled in size and become coed, the officials had built housing on the campus, but the early birds had gobbled up those facilities. Actually, even if there were anything available he wasn't sure he could be happy living in a warren anymore.

The trouble was, he was spoiled. For ten years he and Frannie had owned a brownstone in Brooklyn Heights—not in the choicest part, true, but good enough—and it had provided them rooms to spare.

You can't go home again, he told himself grimly all during the period when he had drifted in and out of furnished rooms; no use trying to recapture the uncapturable.

Frannie had kept the brownstone after their separation. She bore him no animosity; it was she who wanted the separation, and since she could afford to be kind she had let him keep a key to the house and some of his things in the basement. Sometimes when he let himself in he would meet the man who would have been Frannie's next husband if she had lived, and the fellow always complimented him on the paneling he had installed and the special lighting effects he had worked out.

He had enjoyed remodeling the house. All the spare time he'd had those years when he was teaching at Columbia had been given over to the house. Now that Frannie was dead, the house had been put up for sale, but wild horses wouldn't drag him near it, and he couldn't get out of New York fast enough.

That was why he had jumped at the chance of coming to Freebody when Jeff suggested it. Freebody was in eastern Vermont, close enough to New Hampshire so you could see the Presidential Range across the Connecticut River on a clear day. The early houses around the green were imposing, and the families who had inherited them could afford to keep them painted a spruce white. The only sign of commerce and industry was the stone edifice of the Freebody Paper Mill down near the river, but that had been closed now for several years. The college was standing on the original Freebody property; the administration building was the original Freebody house, used before Adam Freebody grew so rich he could build the Castle and give the old place to house the college and the endowment to help it get under way. Except for the problem of housing, Freebody was precisely what Ian needed; it was small, it was country, it was remote, it was the antithesis of New York.

During the two years when he'd been in Vietnam, spending his leisure moments dreaming of coming home to Frannie, she had been growing tired of waiting for him. Even before his return he had become increasingly aware that she no longer felt as happy about their marriage as he did. Still, it was a stunning blow to have his suspicions confirmed, and to learn on his return that she was involved with this other man. He was distraught; he was mad in a controlled way; he was lost. He knew only that he had to obliterate any memory of her from his mind, from their idyllic life together to the last ugly episode of her death.

Jeff told him not to worry about a place to live; something was bound to turn up, and until then he could stay with him and Dodie. He came to Freebody as if he were being pursued. He still woke up at night in a sweat imagining he smelled the stench of burning flesh.

Actually, Jeff and Dodie wouldn't mind if he stayed on in their house. They could have used the money they would have charged him, meals thrown in; but more, he would be welcome for his own sake. Among carefree, good-natured people like Jeff and Dodie, an extra presence wasn't an intrusion. Besides, they had no privacy anyway with three small kids underfoot.

It was Ian who wanted, needed, out. For reasons like his hi-fi, for instance. He couldn't play it as loudly as he liked with the paper-thin walls and one kid or the other being put to bed just when he wanted to turn it on. And Dodie was a terrible housekeeper. He didn't mind keeping the room clean himself, but the mop was too matted with dirt to use, and the vacuum broken, and ever since he had been there he'd heard the running discussion as to whether to fix the vacuum or buy a new one.

She couldn't cook, either. His tastes were simple, but he was fastidious and all too accustomed to meals tastefully served in the brick-floored, candlelit dining room in the brownstone. After an act like that, it wasn't easy to dine in close quarters with three kids brought up permissively. If he had offered to eat out, Dodie would have been hurt. She had the legs of a Rockette, and red hair, but after all, he wasn't enjoying those benefits which made Jeff overlook her housekeeping. Even if he wasn't going to stay at Freebody more than this year, he needed to live somewhere else.

True, the gatehouse was a wreck, but fixing it up would be a project to fill his spare time and take his mind off thoughts of death. Frannie's death gnawed at his guts. The book on medieval fiction which he'd started before Vietnam and to which he longed to get back was bogged down under too heavy a weight of memories, and what he needed was to work with his hands with hammer and paintbrush, to exorcise her.

When he got back to Jeff's house, he found Jeff raking leaves, and he hung around with him, piling leaves in the basket for him, telling him about the gatehouse.

"If you were in my shoes, would you try to speak to the Freebodys?"

Jeff shrugged. "Why not? What have you got to lose? But I doubt they'd even talk to you. Since old Adam died, they don't mix with the town. There's only a daughter left, and the aunt who lives with her, and they phone in orders, or send one of the servants around to shop. The mother was a restless sort who preferred a more sophisticated environment, and the father usually tagged after her."

"What kind of woman is the daughter?"

"I've never seen her." They were carrying the basket of leaves to the back of the house, to the compost heap. "When she was a baby, somebody tried to kidnap her. It made a sensational story, and since then they've had this ex-cop ex-marine guarding the place. He's old now and they've given him other jobs to do, I imagine, now that the daughter is grown up. She must be at least twenty-one."

The ex-cop ex-Marine must have been the man he had met at the Freebody gates this afternoon. Why didn't *he* live in the gatehouse?

"The place is an eyesore," he said. "Odd that they should leave it that way, with all their money."

"There's a story," Jeff said. "I only remember the general details. A boy killed himself in that gatehouse. He was the guard's grandson, and lived there with him. They said the girl, Iris Freebody, was involved some-how. Anyway, after the boy died the old man didn't want to live there, and he moved out to somewhere else on the estate, and they just let the gatehouse fall into ruin."

"Iris Freebody was involved?"

"She didn't kill him, if that's your idea. It was something else. They were supposed to be in love. Maybe it was just a quarrel. They were both very young."

His interest was aroused. "Is she beautiful?"

Jeff grinned. "Not from what I hear. I've never seen her, but Doctor Nichols treats our kids, and he took care of Iris when she had the nervous breakdown after the boy died. He says her mother was a famous beauty around here, but that Iris obviously doesn't take after her. He says she's gawky and plain and abnormally shy, not the sort men kill themselves over. Or boys, for that matter."

"I'm going to telephone her."

"Why not?"

He went into the house. Jeff followed, out of curiosity. Ian was surprised when Information gave him the number; he had been sure it would be unlisted. A man answered his ring, elderly, but not the gatekeeper.

"This is the Freebody house."

"I'd like to speak to Miss Freebody, please."

"Who is calling?"

He was astonished. He hadn't expected to get this far. "My name is Sexton. Miss Freebody doesn't know me." Inspiration seized him. "I'm from the college."

"Freebody College? One moment. I'll see if Miss Freebody will speak to you."

Ian lifted his eyebrows to Jeff as he waited, in disbelief. Minutes later he heard a girl's voice.

"This is Iris Freebody."

"Miss Freebody, my name is Ian Sexton, and I teach

at the college. I'm new this year, and desperate to find a place to stay. I happened to pass your house this afternoon and noticed the gatehouse—"

"What?" she said.

"I wondered if you would rent it to me for the year. I'd be glad to do any and all the repairs myself—"

Suddenly he had the knowledge that there was no one on the line. "Hello?" he said sharply, but no one answered. He held the telephone a minute or two, waiting, feeling like a fool, and was just about to hang up when another female voice came on.

"Yes? Who is this?" the voice asked sharply.

He took a breath and began again. "My name is Sexton and I teach at the college. I wanted to talk to someone about the possibility of renting your gatehouse. I'm very handy, and I would take care of all the repairs so that the place could be lived in—"

The voice at the other end interrupted him. "You must be joking," it said richly. "My niece wouldn't even consider permitting strangers on her estate, and if she wanted the gatehouse repaired she would have seen to it herself. Really, what a ridiculous idea!"

The telephone was put down so emphatically that Jeff heard it. Jeff said, "I gather the answer is no."

"I expected to be turned down, but in a genteel, Boston Back Bay manner," Ian said. "Whoever I spoke to sounded downright vulgar."

"That must have been the aunt. I've run across her in town, and I know what you mean. She's Iris's father's sister, and from what I heard neither was what you'd call genteel. The father was supposed to be

enough of a charmer so that his wife overlooked his
origins, but I've heard that none of his family was
allowed inside the gates until after the mother
drowned in a yachting accident. There was no one to
carry on the Freebody name, and the grandfather insisted that Iris's father change his name to Freebody
when he married Iris's mother, and I guess the marriage was attractive enough to him so that he did. The
aunt only got in to look after Iris when she had a
nervous breakdown, and then the father died and she
just stayed on."

"Would the aunt have anything to say about the
gatehouse, then?"

"I'm afraid so, Ian. The girl seems pretty much
without a mind of her own. Mitchell says she was
always timid, but it was worse after the breakdown."

The gatehouse was out, then. He spent the weekend
looking some more, but he couldn't get the gatehouse
out of his mind, and it spoiled him for anything else.
On Monday classes began, and he resigned himself to
at least another week of Dodie's cooking.

# 2

"**I**ris?"

Her heart leaped in her chest. She had counted on getting out of the house before Aunt Gladys got up, so that when she came back this afternoon college would be an accomplished fact. Why had she awakened so early? "Yes, Aunt Glad?"

"I heard your bath water running, and I wondered what you were doing up at seven o'clock."

She took a deep breath. Tell her through the closed door, it will be easier not having to see her, or let her see you. It is my house, and she is only a guest here, and I am twenty-one and if I decide I want to go to college it is purely my own affair. She knew it all, and reminded herself often, but Aunt Gladys weighed on her.

She steeled herself. "I have to be at Freebody by nine o'clock for my first class. I didn't . . . get around to telling you before. It was sudden, deciding to go. I enrolled last week."

She could almost hear the ponderous silence.

"You're joking, Iris."

"No, I'm not."

"Going to that college, with all the people from town knowing who you are?"

She didn't answer.

"Iris, do you have any idea what you're letting yourself in for?"

"I have to hurry to make the class, Aunt Glad. Can we talk later, when I get back?"

"You're really going ahead with it? You've thought ahead to what it may mean?"

"Yes, Aunt Glad."

"Sometimes I can't figure out what gets into you. You should at least have talked it over with Tieman. Or with Dr. Nichols."

Finally Aunt Gladys went away; she knew because there was no more wheezy breathing outside her door. She told herself again, it's my house and she's only a guest in it. When Ralph and I are married, then she'll be my mother-in-law, and I suppose it will have to be different. But she isn't yet, and even if she were it wouldn't give her the right to make me feel as if I were out of my mind to want to go to school.

But it did no good to remind herself that she was twenty-one and her own woman, and that no one, not even Uncle Bill Tieman, could tell her what to do. Up till she was twenty-one he had been her legal guardian, but now he was only her lawyer and executor, and on the board of the Boston bank that handled her estate. If she had asked him, he would have encouraged her to go to school even if she *was* twenty-one. Aunt Glad watched over her too fussily. The other night when that man had telephoned and Evans had said he was from the college, she had rushed in terror to seize the phone before Aunt Glad. She was acting like a coward, and she would have to tell her eventually, anyway, and there was nothing Aunt Glad could do about it.

But even when she drove to Concord last week to buy clothes for school, she told Aunt Glad she had to see Uncle Bill. Bill Tieman didn't like Aunt Glad, and she didn't like him, so when it was a matter of signing things she often went to Concord to his office. Buying clothes had been another anxiety. She usually ordered things from the New York and Boston catalogues. Mama had bought her clothes when she was at Ames, but Ames had been a small private girls' school, and the girls dressed differently than at Freebody, where she wanted very much to seem like all the others. She could have asked Aunt Gladys, who used to sell dresses at B. Altman in New York, but she didn't want her to know just yet. She wanted to be sure to wear the right thing so that she would be less conspicuous and blend with the student body.

She still didn't know what had given her the courage to go to Dean Bemis's office and register. Maybe it was seeing Ralph leave for Harvard, and knowing the loneliness that would set in, wishing she could get up and go places like Ralph, free as a bird. There was no one now, with Robbie dead, only Aunt Glad closed in her bedroom or in the downstairs sitting room behind a cloud of cigarette smoke, watching her serials on TV; and Coffey, who was undependable since her stroke.

She was never sure how much Coffey understood. And once school started, Ralph didn't come down every weekend, once a month at most, though Boston wasn't that far away.

"Ralph is a very serious boy. He always was, even when he was little," Aunt Glad said. "You can see quick enough he had none of my blood in him. I was never bookish, nor was your father, either, though he was smart enough in other ways, I can tell you. But Ralph's a real student. I know there's nothing he'd want to do more than spend all his time with you, but Harvard Law is no picnic."

Ralph was Aunt Glad's stepson, the child of the husband who'd died after only a few years of marriage and left her Ralph to raise. It was the only thing he *had* left her, Aunt Glad always said, and if she hadn't worked every minute, and had Iris's father to help out, Ralph would never be where he was today, at Harvard Law, and engaged to marry Iris. When Aunt Glad had moved in to be with her after Iris got sick, she had brought Ralph with her, although he was already an undergraduate and only stayed weekends and part of the summer. Iris had been very sick after Robbie's death, and it had been good for her to have Ralph to talk to and go walking with.

But it wasn't only being left alone that had driven her to register. She had brooded for a long time about how ignorant she was, compared to Ralph. Tutors had provided all the education she'd had since she left Ames, and since her illness there hadn't even been tutors.

15

But she hadn't been happy at school. Girls were cruel, as cruel as adults. When she spilled Coke on Frieda's new sweater, Frieda called her ugly, and said she had slits for eyes. All the girls in their room had laughed behind their hands. Miss Ames told her not to be silly, she wasn't ugly at all but had good bones and nice skin to go with her chestnut hair, but she couldn't forget how the girls had laughed. That had been worse even than Frieda telling her that she had slitty eyes.

She knew beauty wasn't everything, but she had grown up in a house where it seemed most important. Everyone always said when they saw her, "Let's hope you grow up to be the beauty your mother is." Mama's picture still hung in the drawing room, accusingly lovely, reminding her that she had failed. Where Mama was tall and graceful, she was only gawky; where Mama could say amusing things, she was humorless, and often tongue-tied.

Now she turned away from the mirror, depressed at her appearance. The slacks were too bright, too new. The sweater ended at an awkward place. She was too long-waisted, the saleslady at the Glad Rag had suggested. She opened her door and peered out. Aunt Gladys was not in sight. Hurriedly she went downstairs and ducked into the breakfast room.

Aunt Gladys was at the table, having her bacon and eggs. "I thought since I was up already, I might as well have breakfast with you. Well, well! Let's see how you look!"

Her glance raked, estimated, appraised. From someone as soft and round as Aunt Gladys you didn't

16

expect such a merciless going-over, but then she had been a saleslady and worked on commission, so maybe she had learned to size people up.

"Very collegiate," said Aunt Glad.

Agnes brought her orange juice. "Just toast and coffee, Agnes, please," Iris said. "I'm late."

"Miss Iris is going to college," said Aunt Glad.

Agnes looked startled. "That should be a nice change for you, Miss Iris. Getting out of the house and all."

"Just remember, you're Iris Freebody, and what anyone says or thinks doesn't matter," said Aunt Glad.

Iris buttered her toast.

"It won't be easy," Aunt Glad said. "They still stop me in the beauty parlor and ask after you. They want to know if you're still sick, if you still blame yourself over that poor boy killing himself. I always tell them that Robbie was unbalanced, but you can see they won't buy that. People believe what they want to believe."

But it wasn't my fault. I didn't know. . . No, she had made her decision already. She knew what people in town thought, how they felt about her. But she had to break free or she was no better than a prisoner in her own house. Ralph never invited her to Boston, or brought his friends here, though she was sure he must have many, so she never got to see anyone, or speak to anyone. She had to make the try, at least.

Uncle Bill said she gave people credit for having longer memories than they really had. He told her it happened five years ago and Robbie was forgotten.

But she knew that people must remember, or why would they bring it up to Aunt Gladys? That letter that had come only a few months ago, that Aunt Gladys had hid in her magazine but which had slipped out when she was going up the stairs. Pink, smelling of perfume. "You couldn't bear to see him love Sally Lucas more. All your money couldn't make you out as pretty as she was, and you knew it, so he had to die." The same words had appeared on other pieces of stationery, but Aunt Gladys was always quick to snatch them from her view.

"I suppose they almost fainted when you showed up at the college," Aunt Gladys said. "I suppose they rolled out the red carpet. Where would that college be without the Freebodys? They must have treated you like royalty."

They were all very nice to me, especially Dean Bemis, and maybe I was naïve to think they would have been just as nice to anyone else. I could even believe that they must have forgotten about Robbie, but maybe they were only careful to act as if they had forgotten about him, because I was a Freebody and they wanted me to be happy there.

Apprehension stirred, like a trembling inside her. No, she would not let it frighten her away.

"Aunt Glad, I feel almost as if this is a beginning for me. Everything is going to change once I go to school. I'll make friends, and get involved with work, and it's going to make me different. It's what I need, Aunt Glad, to get away, out of this house."

"Angel, why do you have to be different? What

could you possibly need? Heavens, you live in a magnificent house, you have all the money in the world, a good-looking boy like Ralph who's going to be a successful lawyer one of these days loves you and wants to marry you. Honestly, Iris, I think you want too much."

Iris covered her sigh with a sip of coffee, and then put down her cup. "I have to go now."

Aunt Gladys followed her out to the hall, caught her and hugged her. She felt Aunt Glad's soft breasts pushing against her, felt her warm, sweet breath like a cow's in her face. She shrank, and Aunt Glad noticed it, and laughed.

"You're so standoffish, angel! What are you going to do after you're married?"

She didn't need to be reminded of that; she thought about it often, and wondered if she would be any good at it. Whenever Ralph kissed her she kept wondering if her face looked even funnier close up, and if he really desired to put his mouth on her mouth. After all, it wasn't a very attractive mouth, and with all the mouths in the world, why should he choose hers? And with hardly any breasts to speak of, why should his hand seek them out? Because of the money. It spoiled his kisses. But Ralph never got angry. He only said of her lack of response, "You'll learn. I can wait." If she had been irresistible, would he have been so willing to wait?

Even her own mother and father hadn't hugged or kissed her, as they might have if she had been pretty and cuddly. When she came to them they seemed to study her as if wondering how two such beautiful peo-

*19*

ple managed to produce such a plain child. They tended to pat her and push her away as if they might stumble over her, and then away they would go to some place more interesting than home, and leave her to Coffey.

But today she wasn't going to think of them, or of Robbie, or of anything bad. This was to be a fresh start, a farewell to her past. She said, "There's Wolfe with the car. See you later."

"Lots of luck, angel. You're a brave girl."

Wolfe had brought Papa's car, which was a two-seater, and old, and wouldn't look conspicuous among the other cars on campus. She had told him she was planning to drive it herself. But as soon as she turned into the traffic at the college gates she realized that the car was more conspicuous than she had thought. People turned around to stare. The car was very low, and had a powerful hum to the motor, and its wheels were wire. Besides, Wolfe kept it too polished. She was relieved when she could park it and walk to her first class.

It went easily. She was elated. At lunchtime another girl asked if she could sit with her. The other girl seemed equally friendless—she had just transferred from State U. Iris went into the bookstore afterward and bought two textbooks, and then strolled to her next class.

The room was crowded, and everyone seemed to know each other, maybe from Orientation Week, which she had shied away from. There was a lot of moving about and changing seats as each new student came in and discovered friends, and she found herself on a little island, with empty seats on both sides. She became aware of her sweater again, too short, and her slacks, too unmistakably new. Everyone else's clothes looked as if they had been unrolled from the bottom of a suitcase.

There was a sudden hush, and the instructor came in. Someone behind her whispered that he was new, that he had taught at Columbia before. He wrote his name on the blackboard: Sexton.

"This is English A-40, a Survey of English Literature, required of all students taking a bachelor's degree, so you may as well stay," he said pleasantly.

He had thinning brown hair and a thin pale face, and a brown moustache which became two sparse parentheses on either side of his mouth and developed into a brown beard. He looked like Iago, or someone out of *The Merchant of Venice*, except that his tweed jacket was unpressed and he wore faded blue jeans under it.

The first thing he did was call for all the class cards, and once he had them he said, "This will seem like a waste of time to you, but I like to associate a name with a face. When I call off your name, would you identify yourself?"

Panic overcame her. In the other classes this morning no one had asked her to identify herself. She sank lower in her seat, her heart beating fast. Remember, you're not going to be afraid of anything anymore. This is a new start, remember.

"Lorman?"

21

"Present."

Someone laughed.

"Press?"

Someone put up his hand.

"Freebody?"

Did she imagine it rang out louder than the others, that people craned to see her, that there was a murmur? "Here," she said in a low voice, blood hot in her face.

He looked at her, and for an instant hesitated. Then, "Marston?"

Gradually her face cooled and her heart beat more quietly. Introductions over, he proceeded with class business, how many papers would be required from them, when exams would be given, which books to buy. That done, he started in on a discussion as to what was literature, and what was its purpose, and she had almost forgotten about the incident of being revealed to all when there was a tap on the door and Dean Bemis looked in, caught Sexton's eye, and Sexton went out into the hall to talk to him.

A buzz of voices rose as he left, loud, strident, fearful. Were they talking about her? She could feel them looking at her. She wished Sexton would come back, so she could be hidden again. She was aware of someone sliding into her row; a girl slipped into the empty seat beside her.

"Imagine your being here. Imagine our being in the same class. You *are* Iris Freebody, aren't you?"

Iris turned and stared into the girl's small, pointed

face; her hair was blond, a wild tangled mass with tendrils over her forehead and in front of her ears.

"Come to think of it, we never did meet face-to-face. Robbie saw to that. He didn't want you to know about me. I'm Sally. Sally Lucas."

The girl's eyes were very bright, her teeth showed behind her pink lips. Her expression was full of hate —and triumph.

Iris stood up. She had a vague feeling that things were falling about her feet, but she didn't wait to see. She pushed past knees to the aisle, and went out without looking back. She heard someone say, "Miss Freebody," and remembered the two blank faces staring after her, Sexton's, Dean Bemis's, and then, her heels clattering in the empty, quiet hall, she achieved the front door and the stone steps and her car parked nose into the shrubs. Somehow she was inside and the motor was racing, somehow she made it home. Leaving the car on the drive for Wolfe to put away, she ran inside.

Aunt Gladys came running out of the sitting room. "Iris? What happened?"

She hurried past her without speaking and up the stairs and into her room, slamming and locking the door. Aunt Gladys followed more slowly, breathing heavily from the climb.

"Open the door, Iris, and tell me what happened!"

She made no sound, and finally Aunt Gladys went away. "That girl is loony for sure," Aunt Gladys muttered, imagining Iris could not overhear.

23

But she did hear. *I'm not loony. And if you think I am, why do you want Ralph to marry me? Does the money make up for my looniness?*

She wasn't loony, only terribly upset. And with reason. Nearing had told her father after Robbie died that if Sally had money she would go to Concord and have her baby in his brother's house, and that she could live there while she raised the baby. Iris's father gave Sally five thousand because Iris begged him to, and because he thought it would help his daughter get better if she didn't worry about Sally and the baby. Only Sally didn't have the baby. She had it aborted.

Iris never dreamed Sally would ever come back to Freebody. How could she foresee that Sally would go to college and be in her class?

Sally hasn't forgotten Robbie any more than I have. She blames me, and hates me, and why shouldn't she?

# 3

*T*he Freebody girl left the classroom almost running. He had only a glimpse of her white, unseeing face, but the thought came that he should catch her before she hurt herself. It was Bemis's look of resignation that stopped him, that and the realization that he couldn't catch her anyway.

"She didn't last very long," Bemis said dryly.

"But she'll be back—don't you think she'll be back?"

"I doubt it very much. I registered her myself because I didn't think she could get through the ordeal with anyone who didn't know her. That's a case of pathological shyness such as I've rarely encountered. I didn't expect her to stick it out, actually, but she *is* a Freebody and the college owes the family a great deal, so I went along with her. I thought she'd stay more than a day, though," he said. "Too bad. I wonder what sent her scurrying off."

Sexton wondered, too. He went back to his class and

noticed a girl sitting next to Freebody's vacant seat, and as soon as the class was over he caught the girl before she could leave.

"Do you happen to know why Miss Freebody left so suddenly? Did anything happen, anyone say anything to her?"

The girl shrugged, her eyes appraising him. "Nothing happened. I just said hello to her."

"Then you know her."

She shrugged again. "Say we had a mutual friend."

"You're—"

"Sally Lucas."

"Sally Lucas. It doesn't sound very alarming." He said it almost as a joke, not meaning anything.

"It means a lot more to her," she said, and her small mouth thinned out. She left, her butt switching in the tight short skirt she wore. He caught his breath. Teaching in a coed school presented distractions. Jeff had warned him that some of the girls sent the single instructors crawling up the walls. And what the devil did she mean by that remark?

On the floor under Miss Freebody's chair he found a notebook, two new textbooks, a monogrammed gold pen and a leather case with glasses. He put them in his desk and at the end of the day he brought them to Bemis.

"She'll probably send someone for these when she remembers they're missing."

"Look," Bemis said, "why don't you run over to the house and bring them back yourself? It'll be a nice gesture." When Sexton hesitated, Bemis added, "You might try and reason her into coming back. You know, encourage her. She did muster the gumption to come here in the first place. Maybe she could be coaxed into coming back for another try."

Even as Bemis was talking, the thought flashed into Sexton's mind: the gatehouse. It would be another chance to talk to her about the gatehouse.

"I might not get past whoever opens the door."

"Tell them you're from the college and you want to speak to her. The college is still something special to the Freebodys, or was, anyway."

So he washed up and brushed the chalk dust from his pants and drove out to the Freebody house. The gates were locked and there was nobody in sight, but he located a buzzer on a post and pressed it. Minutes later someone walked down the driveway. It was the old man he'd spoken to before. Here we go again, Sexton thought resignedly.

"Yes? What's your business?"

"I'm here from the college. To see Miss Freebody." He added quickly, "She's a student of mine."

The gates slid open. The old man watched him as he got back into his car and started up the driveway. The house loomed suddenly in a clearing of lawn and gardens, gray granite, with crenellated turrets and balconies and long narrow windows with leaded glass panes. It was ludicrous, and yet, in its way, overwhelming; all it needed were some sheep grazing in front of the wide stone steps, and maybe a peacock or two spreading their tails languidly, to be an English landscape. He went up the steps and rang the bell. A white-haired man in dark livery opened the door.

"I'm here to see Miss Freebody. I'm Dr. Sexton." He tacked on his academic title uncomfortably, but he knew it impressed people.

He was shown into a large hall where scattered Persian rugs were lost on an expanse of rather grimy marble. A large hearth with stone lion heads supporting the mantle yawned black without a fire. The stairway swept up on two sides, reached a landing and vanished into the gloom above. Tapestries hung on paneled walls, the designs faded by age. On an oak table in the center stood a silver vase that needed polishing, filled with drooping chrysanthemums.

The old man in livery, the first real, live butler he'd ever seen, crossed the hall to a small door and tapped on it. The door opened, emitting a low murmur of television voices, and then a woman came out, small and plump, with a florid face and aggressively gold hair mounded on her head.

"Yes, what can I do for you, Dr. Sexton?"

Her manner was too haughty to be real. He stifled a sigh, and repeated his entrance line.

She nodded stiffly. "I'm Mrs. Forsher, Iris's aunt," she said. "You can leave her things and I'll see that she gets them. Thank you for taking the trouble to come."

She put out her hand, but he stood his ground. He had come this far and he wasn't going to give up so easily. "I'd like to give them to her myself, if I may."

28

She recovered. "You certainly may not! I won't have her reminded again of her unpleasant experience this afternoon! She came home hysterical and won't even open her door! I told her school was no place for her, her being a Freebody, and that dreadful tragedy and all! Iris is very sensitive."

"I'm sorry that anything happened to upset her," he said imperturbably. "It's one of the reasons I came, to try and find out why she was upset and see if maybe I can help."

"You're a very insistent man," she said, her pale eyes bulging at him. "I've already told you that Iris is in no condition to speak to anyone—"

"Aunt Gladys."

The voice came from above. He looked up at a minstrel's gallery carved of stone, with pointed Gothic arches, and saw a shadowy figure in the gloom behind it.

"I can handle him, Iris."

"It's all right, Aunt Glad. Dr. Sexton, will you come upstairs?"

He went past Mrs. Forsher with alacrity, hearing her sharp intake of breath. The door slammed behind her, cutting off the murmur of television voices. He squinted, trying to pierce the shadows of the corridor, and then he made out the figure standing in the faint illumination of an open door.

"Will you come in, Dr. Sexton?"

He entered a dim sitting room, paneled ornately and filled with massive carved pieces. Through an

29

archway he could make out a bedroom, and a tall, wide bed. The dying sunlight came through heavy draperies, lighting a bright swath in the dimness.

"Please sit down."

Her manner was archaically formal, as if it had been absorbed by her through the walls of this house. He felt it was a kind of playacting with her, too, not just to create an effect, as with her aunt, but rather because it was the way she believed she should act.

"This is an interesting room," he said, to fill the silence.

"Do you think so? It was my great-grandfather's, once. I moved into it after my mother and father died."

"You're too young for it."

She started, almost as if he had put a hand on her. "Do you think so? I never thought of that. You see, it's my house now, and it's natural that I should take this room."

"Well, why shouldn't you, if you like it? But I could imagine you in a room with more sun, more light."

"Yes, I suppose you're right. I hadn't thought of it that way."

Silence.

"Well," he said, "now that you're back in school you won't be in your room as much, and it won't matter."

Silence. Then, "I can't go back to school."

He pretended surprise. "Why not?"

"I . . . can't tell you."

"I'm very sorry. I was hoping you would stay."

"Why should you hope that? You don't know me."

He was taken aback. He decided not to beat about the bush, and said briskly, "It would be interesting, having a Freebody in the class. The students would find you interesting, who you are, what you think, what you have to say."

She stared at the pile of books on his lap. He did not want to surrender them yet. Once he did, his tenuous hold on her would be broken. He pretended not to see her stare.

"I was very anxious to go to school," she said slowly. "I'm really uneducated."

It was probably why she had consented to see him, why he was still here. He was her connection with the college, and she did not want to sever it irrevocably.

"Then come back," he said. "Don't let anything put you off." He paused, probing actually. "Or anyone."

"What do you mean?"

Again he chose not to beat about the bush. He wouldn't have fooled her anyway. He was still probing. "I assume it has something to do with that girl in the class. Sally Lucas."

She stared at him, her eyes widening. "How did you know that? Did she say anything about me?"

So he was right. "She only suggested that you and she had some friend in common. I spoke to her after you left because she had been sitting next to you and I thought she might give me some idea why you left in such a tearing hurry."

"She didn't tell you anything?"

31

"That was all."

She looked away. She had long, rather narrow eyes and a very white skin. Somebody who knew about makeup and clothes and hairstyles could make her into a striking figure, but she was woefully unconscious of such artifice, encased in bright plaid slacks and a schoolgirl's sweater.

He said quietly, "Why don't you tell me about Sally Lucas? Maybe we could scotch the bogeyman, and you could go back to class tomorrow."

"It's more than Sally Lucas. It's . . . everybody."

"You mean it's everybody knowing you're a Free-body, and a benefactor of the school?"

"I'd already made up my mind that I wasn't going to let that bother me. But. . ." She stopped.

He said again, "Why don't you tell me? I'm a stranger, and it's easy to talk to strangers. People tell the most intimate details of their lives to strangers, because they know they won't see one another again. Since you don't plan on coming back to school, which means we aren't likely to meet again, why don't you tell me?"

She got up abruptly, almost distraught. "It's getting dark. I didn't notice. I should turn on the lamps."

"Don't turn them on yet. It's nice this way."

She turned her head to look at him. "Yes, it *is* nice. I thought . . . how nice it was." She hesitated. "It's the only place I ever feel . . . private. It makes it . . . easier to talk."

"Good. Tell me about Sally Lucas, why don't you."

Again her glance was quick, and searching somehow. His face in the dimness, his quiet, seemed to reassure her; her words came in a rush.

"Robbie was Nearing's grandson. Nearing is our gatekeeper. When he came to work for us he brought Robbie with him to live, so we practically grew up together. Someone tried to kidnap me when I was a baby, you see, and so I wasn't allowed to go anywhere after that, and I didn't have any friends except Robbie. I did go to school for a while, but I wasn't happy there. My aunt says I have trouble getting along with people."

"How do you know, if you're never *with* people?"

She hesitated, frowning, but seemed to decide to consider what he said later; she could not stop now. Again her words were a torrent.

"Robbie asked me for a thousand dollars. We were very close, so he would ask me. We had even talked about getting married. I was sixteen and he was eighteen, so we were too young, but I did think we might, one day. I thought . . . we were in love. I would have gladly given him the thousand dollars, but I didn't have it."

She flushed, and even in the by now exhausted light her face seemed to bloom with color. He was afraid to speak, afraid to encourage her to go on. She spoke to him as if he were a faceless shadow, but friendly somehow, and he did not want to remind her of his reality.

"I would have done anything for Robbie! I would

33

have given him the money if I had it! My father was in Europe, and I was supposed to go to Uncle Bill Tieman who was then the family lawyer, not my guardian yet, not until my father died, if there was anything I needed. When I went to Uncle Bill he said just because I was rich I mustn't be irresponsible with money, and to be on my guard against people who would pretend to be my friends but who were only using friendship as a way to get my money. I didn't know what to do! I begged Robbie to go to his grandfather, but he was afraid. I think Nearing was harsh with him, even hit him sometimes. He was very strict with Robbie, and stronger than Robbie, and Robbie was afraid of him. And I still didn't know why Robbie couldn't say what he needed the money for. Not yet."

Her voice shook so badly that he became alarmed. Maybe it was the wrong thing to dredge up the past, maybe it did no good to talk about it, maybe it offered no relief for her. He had no idea what he was about to stir up, and now he listened uneasily.

"I never knew the money was for Sally Lucas!" she cried. "I never knew he had made her pregnant! If I knew I could have told Uncle Bill and he would have given me the money, but he probably thought it was just for something like a car, or a present I wanted to give Robbie, something silly, I don't know! Even Coffey told me she would have managed the money for him if she had known. But he wouldn't tell anyone! He was afraid! I never found out until it was too late."

Too late. The boy was dead. In the gatehouse.

She said, her voice a breath, "I went looking for him. I used to stop by the gatehouse for him. Nearing was always busy somewhere else, so we met there." The breath died altogether. He barely heard her. "He was . . . he was hanging from the closet door. I found him."

She shuddered, and covered her face with her hands.

He was shocked into silence himself. "Horrible," he said finally. "And how ghastly for you." *I never found Frannie; others did. But I imagine how she must have looked.* He lifted his shoulders and let them fall, trying to dispel his own images, capsulizing what she had said, sealing it, marking it over and done with, the past.

But she wouldn't let him. "I will never forget him."

"You must. It's horrible, and tragic, but you had nothing to do with her pregnancy or his suicide, and you mustn't let it haunt you for the rest of your life."

"People in town think I had something to do with it. I didn't give him the money."

"How do you know people think that? After all, you were a kid of sixteen."

"Aunt Glad told me. Ralph told me. They didn't tell me directly, but I surmised it, from what they didn't tell me. I'd see the letters before they began to hide them from me. The letters said I was jealous because Robbie loved Sally more than me, and so I wanted him to die."

"Are you sure Sally didn't write those letters to you herself?"

She looked at him speechless. "Sally! I never thought—"

"It's just a guess. She just might be that kind of person, you don't know. And then there may be a raft of people who would enjoy tormenting you. Sick people. Crackpots."

"People must hate me even without what happened to Robbie. The mill closed, and a lot of people were thrown out of work. My father got sick and there was no one to run it. . . . I don't like to go into town for that reason. I feel the hate in them. Aunt Gladys tells me how people make remarks about the family to her, veiled remarks."

"Your aunt tells you that. Now why should she repeat anything like that to you?" She did not answer, and he did not pursue it. "But you're not going to hide out here all your life because of some crackpots? Are you going to let sick people deprive you of the education you want?"

For a moment he thought he had reached her. But then she said, "I can't face Sally Lucas. She said she wanted to go away and have her baby and never come back, but she changed her mind and had the abortion, and it's inevitable that I would have to run into her on campus, sometimes, somewhere."

"Face her," he said. "Face her every day, get used to it, and be a free woman. Come back to school."

Her voice shook. "I can't. I just can't."

She said it so intensely that he knew there was no point in arguing further. This time when she rose to turn on the lamps he let her. Her tall figure moved stiffly; she stumbled on the rug once, as if she were

36

self-conscious about his watching her. She sat down again in the same chair.

"What makes it sad is that you want the education."

She agreed in silence, the slope of her shoulders echoing her despondency. But she did not get up and give him his cue to go. It was as if she wanted him to stay. If he stayed, some opening might come up, some way for him to bring up the gatehouse. He couldn't now; it would be too crude. He was thinking all the while, and said at last, tentatively, "I wonder if they would give you college credit if an instructor were to come here from the school to tutor you."

She looked up. "I don't want to be tutored. I had tutors, when I was sick. I'm not sick anymore."

"Suppose something could be arranged," he said, thinking out loud. "You're already enrolled in my class. Suppose I were to arrange to come here once or twice a week to keep you up to date with the work we're doing. Then as the term wore on, and you felt more confidence, about Sally Lucas and the others, you could just slip back into the classroom."

Her mouth parted as if he had given her new hope. "That would be wonderful—" Suddenly her eyes searched his face. "Why should you go to so much trouble?"

It was the opening he had been looking for, but he still couldn't bring himself to say it: it would be no problem at all, if he lived in the gatehouse. Instead he said, "It wouldn't be trouble, especially if I didn't live too far away. I haven't found a place yet, but—"

She drew back. "It was you who called about the gatehouse."

Damn! Whatever he had gained would now be lost. He nodded.

She said, "Is that why you came here today, to ask about the gatehouse?"

He would lose, but so would she, if he did not temper the truth. "I came because I was curious to know why a student of mine should run out without any apparent reason, and because you left your things behind. Here they are. You may as well take them."

She took them silently and put them on the desk.

"I came also because Dean Bemis asked me to. He was hoping you would come back. And so was I. He might have asked me to make some inquiries whoever you were, not just because your name is Freebody. Maybe it did mean more, because you are a Freebody." She didn't say anything, and he went on, "Offering to teach you was a spur-of-the-moment thing. I honestly didn't have it in my mind when I came here." He added, "I'd like you to believe me."

She whispered, "I wish the gatehouse would disappear. I should have had it torn down, right away."

"I can understand."

So that was that. He started to get up, when, as if following some secret cue, the aunt's voice was heard outside.

"Iris? Is everything all right?"

The girl flushed, and for an instant her eyes met his

in embarrassment. He made a face, and she smiled, and it was as if a bond had been formed between them, the two of them against the intruder. He felt emboldened enough to say under his breath, "Tell her you're being violated."

Her flush deepened, but the smile still flickered. "Everything is all right, Aunt Glad."

The aunt's footsteps retreated back down the stairs. He hoped he hadn't gone too far. He said, "Does your aunt live with you all the time?"

"She's only been here since I got sick. My father thought I should have someone in the family with me, and there was no one else. My mother died before, and my father already had cancer and knew he would be dead within the year. He was never close to Aunt Glad, and hardly saw her when my mother was alive, but he left her a small income if she would stay with me as long as I needed her. I don't really need her anymore, but she thinks this is her home. Coffey, who brought me up, had a stroke a few years ago and isn't much help now. But you see, there was Ralph. Ralph is Aunt Glad's stepson. He was already in college when she came to stay with me, and he only lives here weekends and summers. It was wonderful to have someone near my own age after . . . after Robbie. Ralph and I are engaged."

"You're engaged?" He was too surprised to think of anything else to say. He couldn't imagine she knew any man well enough to be engaged. "Congratulations. When are you getting married?"

"When Ralph graduates from law school, in June. It isn't official, of course. I mean, there hasn't been any announcement. My aunt and Ralph both think it's better this way, so there won't be the publicity, and people won't begin writing those awful letters again."

He was still recovering from his astonishment. "Ralph's a lucky man."

She looked at him soberly. "Because he'll be rich?"

"That, too. I wasn't thinking of the money. He's lucky because you're a very nice young woman."

"You don't know me."

"It's an educated guess."

"Ralph is very attractive. I'm not pretty."

"Who said that? I think you're attractive."

He said it as much out of kindness as honesty, because he could see it was of more than casual importance to her. Most girls would have smiled and let it go at that, but she looked at him soberly. "Please don't say things to please me. You don't have to. Not to stay in the gatehouse. I'll have to think about the gatehouse, about someone living in it again. I'm not sure I can ... I can bear it yet. Telling me I'm attractive won't change that."

He felt a real flash of anger, so that he hardly noticed the mention of the gatehouse. "I'd like to wring the neck of whoever gave you that low opinion of yourself."

It was as if his sincerity reached her. Color came up again in that white skin.

He had meant what he said; damn it, she was a hell

of a lot more interesting to look at than those inane vapid faces that everyone rated as pretty.

She said, "Why do you want the gatehouse?"

He was disconcerted, but he managed to come up with the reasons.

"It needs so much work."

"It's one of the reasons I want it. I'd like to work on it. It's cheaper than therapy."

"Do you need therapy?"

He said lightly, "Someday I may explain that. By the way, will you want to go ahead with my suggestion about the lessons?"

"Even if you don't live in the gatehouse?"

"Even if I don't live in the gatehouse."

She got up thoughtfully to show him out, without giving him an answer. They went downstairs together. Standing at the front door with her, he happened to look up and saw at the top of the stairs an old woman looking down at him. He could not see her clearly but she seemed to be bent, and leaned on a cane for support. For an instant the memory flashed back to him of his first glimpse of the Freebody place, and how he had half expected to see a witch come out of the gatehouse bending over her gnarled stick. His face must have reflected his thoughts, because Iris noticed his expression and glanced upward.

"It's all right, Coffey," she called. To him she said, "That's Miss Coffey. She still watches over me as if I were a child."

The old woman stared down at him, motionless. He

felt her glance as sharp as an eagle's, in spite of her frailty.

"I would like to take the lessons," Iris said. "If you still want to give them."

"I do," he said. "Give me a week or two to get settled somewhere. But you have the textbook, and you can begin reading."

She said, "I'll make up my mind about the gatehouse. I'll think about it. It would be so much easier for you if you could stay in it and not have to drive any distance, especially in the winter."

He opened the door.

"I'll call you. Will it be all right to leave a message in the English office, when I . . . when I decide?"

"That will be fine."

He walked down the stairs and out to his car. She's going to give the gatehouse to me, he thought. He was oddly sure. He suppressed his excitement until he was clear of the gates, and then he let it out in a shout. Plans teemed in his head. He'd have the glazier first, to make the house weathertight. Then lumber and paint and stain; he'd do that himself. Check the wiring; check the plumbing; the roof. These old houses were built to last, and he didn't foresee any real difficulty. He'd have it tight as a drum before winter. Pleasant images came to him, of winters with Frannie— No. Forget that. Don't think of Frannie. There were two chimneys in the gatehouse, which meant fireplaces. Bach would fill his house by Christmas. Shelves for all his books. Quiet. No one to pass those electrically controlled gates and barge in. The stinging cold air of Vermont when he opened his windows.

*If* she let him have it.

She *would* let him have it. An obscure sense told him so. What he couldn't imagine was how long Iris had stood by the open door, watching his car until it was lost to sight.

# 4

*S*he knew with a heavy heart that there was no avoiding Aunt Glad; they had to meet at dinner.

"The colossal brass of that man," said Aunt Glad. "Forcing his way in here on a phony excuse that he had to return books to you. I practically told him to leave, and I would have stood my ground if you hadn't interfered."

"But he did have something to tell me."

"He forced himself on you is how I'd put it."

Iris took a deep breath. It was strange how from the moment she had called down to him to come upstairs, through his visit in her rooms with the door shut securely, she had begun to feel mistress of the house, not just know it, but *feel* it. It made her able to say, "If anyone comes to see me from now on, Evans will tell me who it is, and I'll make up my mind if I want to see him or not."

For a minute Aunt Gladys was wordless. She said,

"Well!" under her breath, and tightened her mouth. "If you want to put yourself at the mercy of any unscrupulous person who will know how to take advantage of you, then—then I can't stop you, I'm afraid."

*But you take advantage of me, too, Aunt Glad.* Ever since Coffey had to give up the household accounts, Aunt Gladys had done them, and it would be humiliating to her if Iris were to ask for them back. Aunt Gladys said it made her feel better, being useful. But Coffey was always hinting about *why* it made her feel better. That check Iris had signed to do the stonework. It still had never been done. Neither had a lot of other things for which she had signed checks. If more and more money was needed for the housekeeping, well, prices had gone sky high, Aunt Gladys said. Still, even Bill Tieman had remarked on their rocketing expenses and asked if they were dining on plovers' eggs and hummingbirds' tongues. Coffey said Aunt Gladys was feathering her nest. The annuity that papa had set up for Aunt Glad was hardly enough to suit her new style of life; Iris had already asked Uncle Bill to increase it after she and Ralph were married and Aunt Gladys moved away. So let the old girl feather her nest meanwhile, if she wanted to. Iris simply refused to hurt her by taking over the accounts herself, and besides she didn't want to be bothered with them. It just meant Aunt Glad bought herself another color TV or went on another Caribbean cruise when she caught cold and said she couldn't shake it in this terrible climate. Aunt Glad always invited her to come along,

*45*

but Iris never went. She didn't want to face hordes of strangers yet. When she married Ralph it would be different.

Now she said, "Aunt Glad, who has the keys to the gatehouse?"

"Nearing, I suppose. Why?"

She took a breath. "Dr. Sexton said he would like to fix it over and stay in it this year. I've been thinking—"

"Dr. Sexton live in the gatehouse!" Aunt Gladys's eyes bulged.

"I haven't said he could. I'm thinking about it. He's going to come here one or two nights a week to teach me—"

"So that's how he wangled it!" Aunt Gladys sat back. "He offered to teach you, which meant he'd be coming here and doing you a favor, so how could you refuse?"

"I haven't said yes, Aunt Glad. I want to think some more. The gatehouse *is* there. I see it. It isn't as if we had it torn down. Maybe it might be better if it were fixed up; maybe it's worse now because it's so desolate, so ... dead. Maybe I would even mind it less if it didn't look so ... so haunted."

"Of all the brass!" said Aunt Gladys. "So that's why he wormed his way into this house—"

"He didn't worm his way into the house, Aunt Glad. He just came to return my things and ask me to come back to school. He only offered to teach me when I told him I wasn't going back to Freebody. It was very nice of him to offer—"

"Nice of him," said Aunt Gladys, shaking her head.

"Oh, what a child you are, Iris! Anyone can tell you anything, and you're taken in! Don't you see his game? Why should he want to live in that wreck, and come here to teach you? He has his reasons, you can be sure, and the next thing you know he'll be taking other steps—"

"Aunt Glad, we don't know what his reasons are," she said, although Aunt Gladys's words were like little knives stabbing away. Why *should* he want the gatehouse? Why should he offer to teach her? Why should he be interested? He didn't know her. "But whatever they are, I do want to get an education. A person my age should know so much more than I do. Dr. Sexton taught at Columbia before and he seems very intelligent. I could learn a lot from him. It would be awful when Ralph and I are married if we can't talk together on the same level."

"Young people have plenty to amuse themselves with besides having intellectual conversations," said Aunt Gladys. But it was obvious she had been mollified, reassured, by Iris's mention of the marriage. "Just be on your guard all the time is my advice to you." She buttered some bread. "Ralph isn't going to like it at all, you spending your evenings with a strange man, maybe even having him live on your estate."

"I don't see why he should mind my getting lessons."

"Getting lessons," said Aunt Glad. "And from a man who looks as suspicious as that one."

"Suspicious?"

"Just look at him. Looks like Satan, with that face. I

never trusted a man with that kind of moustache and beard. Villainous. And those penetrating eyes, looking right through you."

"I didn't notice."

"That's what I mean about you, Iris. You're inexperienced in the world. Oh, you can't help it, I know, what with people wanting to kidnap you since you were an infant and having to be shut up here because people are mean and think things about you, but what chance do you have against a smart schemer?"

Iris had thought Dr. Sexton rakish and somewhat careworn, as if he had lived hard and not always happily, and there was something behind his eyes, something ... But he wasn't suspicious-looking. He had managed to get her to think about the gatehouse because he was kind, and intelligent, and interesting, and because it seemed to mean so much to him that it was hard to refuse him. Why *should* she refuse him? Why shouldn't she let him live there if he wanted to?

She went upstairs to her room. Opening the French doors she walked out onto her little stone balcony and stared over the massed shrubs toward the roof of the gatehouse. Yes, it would be better if the chimneys were sending up puffs of smoke, if there were someone nice sleeping there, eating there, ridding the house of its ghosts with his warm, live presence.

The next morning she telephoned the English Office and left a message for Dr. Sexton. The gatehouse was his; he was to ring at the gates and ask Nearing for the keys.

That afternoon Aunt Gladys told her that Ralph

would be driving up for the weekend. Aunt Gladys must have put the situation very dramatically, because Ralph was always hard-pressed for time, not only because he had to study but because he had a part-time job clerking in a law office. It was flattering that Ralph would be worried enough about her spending a few hours a week with Dr. Sexton to drop everything and come here, but it was annoying that Aunt Gladys should have sent for him. Sometimes she felt as if she were some captive goose that Aunt Glad was tending and fattening up for the kill.

The kill. Unexpectedly, she shivered. Now why should such a thought even have crossed her mind?

"Going to have your hair done in the beauty salon in town, angel?" asked Aunt Glad.

Iris shook her head.

"I know how you feel, poor angel. All those tongues going a mile a minute. Well, you're natural, and that's nice, too. Ralph will love you even if your hair isn't done."

*Ralph will love me if I look like a witch, because I will still be a rich witch.* No, that was unfair to Ralph. Ralph didn't have to marry her. One day Ralph would be successful, and rich on his own. He was ambitious and a hard worker, determined to get ahead. He must like her a little. Sexton's words came back to her. He had said he would like to wring the neck of whoever gave her such a low opinion of herself. She could still hear the anger in his voice when he said it.

In her room that night she found herself studying her image in the mirrors. When Mama had taken over this bedroom she had lined the walls with closets for all her clothes, and the closet doors with mirrors. When the mirrored doors were opened strategically, one could lie in bed and see oneself from many varied angles. She could imagine why Mama would want to view herself from so many angles when she was in bed with Papa, but would Ralph be interested in her that way, too? No, she did not think so. Ralph would probably close the closet doors and turn out the lights, out of consideration for her sensitivity. Mirrors would be for other women, in other rooms. She let out her breath in a sigh, and turned away, and went out onto her balcony.

There was a light in the gatehouse. Sexton was there.

Her heart leaped, and began to pound. Was he only looking around, or was he actually planning to sleep there, amid such desolation?

She had trouble falling asleep, thinking of him there, and she was out of bed early in her nightgown to see if there was smoke coming from one of the chimneys. There was not, but even as she looked she saw his car back out and the gates open to let him on his way. He had stayed there all night!

Later in the morning a glazier's truck came. The leaves were already sparse enough for her to see through the trees and watch someone at work on the windows. A lumber truck came and dropped off boards, and then Shepp's Market truck made a stop at the gatehouse before it delivered the groceries to the castle. He must be planning to eat there tonight.

Coffey would be wondering what was happening. Iris hadn't had the chance yet to run upstairs and tell her about deciding to let Sexton use the gatehouse, but Coffey could see the activity from her bedroom window. She went up now and tapped on Coffey's open door.

"It's me, Coffey."

Coffey was often confused, since her stroke, and one could never be quite sure of the state in which one would find her. Sometimes she got around nimbly with her cane, and sometimes she had to stay in her chair, just as there were times when her mind was just as sharp as ever and other times when her mind was completely vague.

As Iris had guessed it would be, Coffey's chair was pushed close to the window, and Coffey was peering out.

"What's going on down there?"

Iris explained about the gatehouse and Sexton.

Coffey listened intently, saying only, "Well! So you got yourself a tenant!" But moments later she seemed to lose track and seized her hand. "Iris, you haven't any plans to send me away to a home? I could still do useful work if you'd let me. I'd die in one of those homes."

"Why do you even bring that up now, Coffey? Haven't I told you this will always be your home?"

"Once you marry Ralph, she'll take over, and you won't be mistress here anymore. She will. Wait and see."

Coffey distrusted Aunt Gladys. It wasn't Aunt

Gladys who had usurped Coffey's position in the house, it was the stroke, but Coffey tended to get the sequence confused, and blamed Aunt Gladys. Coffey thought she could still handle the accounts; she didn't realize how unreliable her arithmetic had become. Certainly Coffey had run the house better than Aunt Gladys; the maids had been more scrupulous, and Evans used to do the silver with some regularity. Aunt Gladys was lazy, and the servants didn't respect her the way they had Coffey, and so there were the dust whorls blown into the corners, and spiders lacing their webs around the chandeliers.

"Sexton won't stay more than a year, I'm sure. I wonder if Aunt Gladys would like to live in the gatehouse after Ralph and I are married."

"You'll never get her off your backs. She's a leech." Coffey reached into a jar and selected a piece of candy, then offered the jar to Iris. "That fellow in the gatehouse worked a good part of the night. I watched him through my binoculars. He was on the roof with a flashlight. Then he put out all the furniture. Planning to get rid of it. Nearing must have told him none of it was his, and he didn't want any part of it."

She hadn't dreamt of the gatehouse last night, or of Robbie's torn sneakers dangling like the feet of a rag doll. She had been sure she was going to dream of it, after seeing the place lighted up. But it was as if Sexton's presence had laid the other to rest. She said, "Ralph's coming this weekend."

"What brings him around? Ain't even a holiday."

She laughed. That was Coffey's way of speaking

about anyone she didn't care for, and she didn't care for Ralph just because he was related to Aunt Glad. "I think he's coming to check up on Dr. Sexton. He wants to be sure I'll be safe with him."

Coffey said sharply, "Anything wrong with this Sexton?"

"Of course not. He just isn't what you'd expect a professor to look like, but I guess styles in professors have changed."

"You seem glad about his coming here."

Iris hesitated. Glad? "I suppose I'm interested in studying with him. The college said I could get credit for the course if I fulfilled the other requirements."

"You should have stayed at college, Iris. You shouldn't have let anything scare you away."

"Dr. Sexton said that, too. I'm going to try again."

"You always did let people scare you. You let your aunt rob you blind, conniving with the shopkeepers, asking for money for jobs that never get done. Didn't she get money to have the stonework checked? When your grandfather was alive it was checked every year. I didn't see the masons this year."

"I'll remind her. Don't worry about it, Coffey."

"You're afraid of her, Iris. You're afraid she'll go off and take Ralph with her. But you needn't be. They've got their claws in you and they'll never let you go until everything is theirs. Just make sure you don't sign anything until Mr. Tieman approves. You're marrying a lawyer, and it will be easy for him to trick you. When they take over, we'll both be without a roof over our heads."

53

"Coffey, you mustn't worry so much. And anyway, you shouldn't talk about Ralph that way. I love him and I'm going to marry him."

"You're like the princess in those stories I used to read to you, who got waked up with a kiss and fell in love right away. What do you know about love? He's the only man who ever kissed you, so you think you're in love. I'm afraid for you, Iris. I'm afraid for you to fall in their clutches." She was beginning to whimper, tears working out from between her eyelids, which meant she was off again. Iris found a tissue and put it into her hand. She would be confused for a while, as if a shade had been pulled down over a window and shut out the light. She made sure Coffey's glass of milk was where she would not tip it over, and let herself out.

The house seemed too dark, too old. She should have more sun and light, Sexton said. She had a craving to breathe, to be outside in the limitless, winy air. The house was like a mantle of stone, pressing down on her, cramping her lungs. If only Ralph didn't love it so; he wanted to continue to live in it after they were married. "It's unique, Iris. It's a castle. How many people do you know who would turn down the chance to live in a castle?"

I would. I can't breathe in it sometimes. I only feel good when I'm out of it. But Ralph thinks that's morbid of me. He thinks I'm still sick and that's why I react to it this way. But I'm not sick, I'm not. Just shy of people, that's all.

Ralph says he dreams of the day when he can live

here. Does he dream of living here with me? Does he dream of me, ever?

Troubled, she found herself taking the path to the gatehouse, as if there were an answer there. Its peaked slate roof loomed through the trees, and the crisp air was tinged suddenly with the smell of fresh paint.

Sexton was outside, with a paintbrush in his hand. She stood some distance away, watching him, timid about announcing her presence until he became aware of her. He was wearing a paint-stained sweat shirt over his jeans and was spattered with fine drops of white paint like confetti, even his moustache and beard. He beckoned her with his paintbrush.

"You look like a dryad, in that green sweater."

She didn't know whether he was serious, or how to answer him.

"You always have to paint over fresh putty, or it dries out," he said, ignoring her speechlessness. "In a day or two this will be ready for the second coat."

She found her voice. "Are you really living in there?"

He grinned. "Call it camping out. But the water's running, and the heat is on, and I've got a mattress and a bottle of Montrachet in the refrigerator, which is now plugged in and working. If you wait until I finish this window, I'd like you to come in and have a glass with me, to toast the work in progress."

She shrank. No. No, she couldn't. Even now in the crisp late afternoon, with the new windows blazing copper in the sun, and the absurd figure that he made, even now beyond the door a desperately unhappy specter lingered, frightened enough to want to die. Hear the bare floors creak under her feet again, hear her voice calling "Robbie?" but no answer. . .

"Not ready yet?" he asked quietly.

She shook her head.

"There'll be other times," he said, his hand steady as he laid an even line of paint over the putty. "I hope your aunt was agreeable about my moving in."

She glanced at him quickly, to meet his amused eyes. She said with dignity, "It *is* my house."

She stayed until it grew too dark for him to continue, and he wiped his brush and put it into a can he had labeled with a magic marker: turpentine. He was so methodical, so careful in his work that it was pleasant watching him, not only to admire his competence, but also his contentment.

He walked her to the driveway. "I can't tell you how grateful I am for your letting me stay here."

"Are you really?" She flung out her hands awkwardly. "But you've taken on so much work. Could I send someone to help?"

"I told you, the work is partly why I'm grateful. This has been the best day I've had in a long time."

*Why?*

"I hope you'll come again," he said. "The wine will always be there for the day you make up your mind to walk in."

The next afternoon she was on the balcony, watching for the gates to open and his car to come through. Her heart bounded. There he was! She marked time, measuring the moments he'd need to put his things away or change his clothes or look around a bit before he started work, and then she walked down the drive to the gatehouse, making herself meander leisurely so he couldn't guess her eagerness.

This time the front door was open and he was whitewashing the hall. He called out, "Come in and have a look. I was at the living room and bedroom walls till two this morning."

"I'll just stand here," she said. She leaned on the doorjamb. Nearing's musty old-man smell was gone, blown away through the open windows. Now there was only the smell of paint, with maybe a lingering memory of the mice and chipmunks who had shared the house and who must have stayed on while the house was tenantless. She told Ian about the chipmunks in the attic. "Robbie and I played here when we were kids, and we'd hear them scampering about over our heads. Their claws would go scratching on the floor so lightly and fast."

"I noticed some holes they may have made. I'd better fill them up," he said. "I like the thought of chipmunks in the attic, but I'd hate them to gnaw at my stereo wiring, or my books." He went on without turning his head, "Sounds as if you had some great times in this house."

"We did. We—" Suddenly, she wept. She turned and walked back to the house, because she couldn't stop crying. At the steps she paused and let the wind dry her face.

*She would bring picnic lunches, and they would*

*make a fire in the fireplace to roast potatoes, and pretend they were pioneers in a log cabin. It was great, great, until . . . It was always fun, waiting for school to be over and Robbie to be home, and hurrying to the gatehouse. Sometimes Nearing would return unexpectedly, and they would hide, cowering in a closet, not daring to breathe, and they would listen to Nearing and stifle their laughter when they heard him talking to himself, or taking a can of beer out of the refrigerator, or lowering himself with a deep grunt onto his bed. They would climb out of the window and run blindly across lawns and fields, flinging themselves down on the ground streaming with perspiration, laughing wildly.*

Remembering, she found herself smiling.

The door was open when she came back the next day, and she could hear him somewhere inside, whistling.

"Dr. Sexton?" He did not hear her. She took a tentative step over the threshold. "Dr. Sexton?"

"In the kitchen!"

She took a deep breath. *Yes. I will. Now.* She went through to the kitchen, not looking right or left. The kitchen was white and smelled of soap powder and new boards. She exclaimed. "I never thought it could look so nice!"

"This is only the beginning. I may panel that wall if there's any shelving left over. The plaster is pretty far gone."

"You don't have any furniture."

58

"I'll buy what I need. Just the essentials."

"But you have nothing to sleep on!" Nearing had made a few trips for Sexton with one of the estate trucks and carted away everything Sexton had put out, even Nearing's broken-down bedstead.

"I have a new box spring and mattress. Want to see?"

She drew away, feeling the blood leave her face.

He said, "There's no one there. It's another room now. My room."

Gently he took her arm and led her inside, past the dazzling white and empty living room where new shelves of pine were beginning to climb around the fireplace, past a scrubbed bathroom, and when her steps faltered he seemed to draw her on, into the bedroom that Robbie had shared with Nearing. Whiteness, and bare walls and floor, the green thick branches of pine rustling outside the open windows, scenting the room. On the floor was his new spring and mattress, and a pine board propped on two stacks of brick, where he had put a typewriter and his briefcase.

"See?"

She nodded. Even so she did not want to stay there.

"Will you have the wine today?"

She nodded again, and they went back into the kitchen, where he took the white wine from the refrigerator and poured it into two paper cups.

"To my new house, and the girl who made it all possible."

She sipped the wine, hiding her flush of pleasure. "I think I see why you enjoy working here. It's like a transformation. Like making something wonderful out of nothing."

"It wasn't exactly nothing. I could see the possibilities. It was just the superficial things that had to be done to it."

"You said it was therapy. Why do you call it therapy?"

"Ah, that's a long story," he said. "Let's just say that it's easy to forget everything when you're planing a piece of wood, or trying to get a shelf plumb. Or even scrubbing a tub."

She said, "I suppose that's one kind of therapy I'll never be able to make use of. I mean, we'll probably live in the house for the rest of our lives, and people will always take care of it for us."

"Poor little rich girl," he answered her lightly, until he saw her expression, and then he said more seriously, "I'm only teasing. I know perfectly well that agony can exist in high and unlikely places, and I can see that the last few years were very painful for you. But now you have to put that behind you, don't you? You're in love with an attractive young man, and he with you, and you are going to get married."

He wants to marry me, but is he in love with me? She wished she could say it, but it sounded so . . . so foolish. She looked at Sexton, and saw his brows drawn together in inquiry, as if he were surprised that she did not respond. "Yes, I suppose so."

"You suppose so?" He sounded mildly astonished.

She stumbled, "I mean, how do you know if it's

right, if you're both right for each other? You *think* you are—"

"What other reason would there be to marry, unless it was something you wanted desperately, and couldn't be happy without?" His face sobered, and became remote suddenly. He said, "I was married once. I loved my wife. Love, passion, it doesn't matter what you call it. I knew that love was in my pores, in my breath, in every sleeping and waking moment. I couldn't imagine life without her. I was . . . someone new and different, loving her."

She hardly dared ask. She breathed, "What happened?"

He lifted his shoulders, and let them fall. "She's dead. She was killed. An accident." He shook his head brusquely as if to dispel an image. "I don't want to remember. It's why I'm here, why I enjoy working on the gatehouse."

*What kind of an accident? Did she love you, too, the same way? You never said.*

But love with Ralph was different. She liked to be with him, she liked the way he walked, slope-shouldered and intent, she liked the shape of his head and the way the hair grew low on his forehead, she liked to touch him and be close to him. She waited eagerly for his coming, as if he opened a door for her to a large, bright, happy world. The feelings would be deeper once they made love, but Ralph was being careful about that because of her breakdown after Robbie, and he did not want to push her until he was

**61**

sure she was ready. And he did work very hard. Harvard Law was a grind, everyone knew that, and the competition was fierce, and he wanted to graduate in the top percent of his class because he said it would determine which firms offered him jobs. How could you surrender to love and passion when there were all these pressures? After they were married, it would be different. Wouldn't it?

She frowned. "Not everybody can love the same way. Some people are able to feel more deeply than others." She felt herself flounder at his quizzical look. "I mean—myself, for instance. How could I know?"

"From the little I know you," he said, "I would judge that you feel intensely about almost everything."

She felt her face grow warm, and tried to laugh. "Coffey says I'm like the girl in the fairy tale who fell in love with the first man who kissed her."

"I don't believe that. That would be a terrible mistake."

Suddenly she was overwhelmed by uncertainty, as if the clear light ahead had clouded, and she was groping again. Maybe it was coming back here to the gatehouse, and Robbie, that made her feel lost. "I have to get back," she said faintly, moving away from him. "Aunt Gladys likes to watch a program at seven-thirty, and we try to finish dinner before." She crumpled her paper cup and put it in the sink.

He walked her to the driveway. It was already dark outside, and the lamps that led to the house were lighted.

"I've upset you," he said, because she remained silent. "Or was it the house?"

She shook her head.

"Let me walk you home."

She shook her head again, and so vehemently that he lifted his eyebrows. She could not tell him that she didn't want Aunt Gladys to see them together, that Aunt Gladys would jump at once to the wrong conclusions. She said, "Don't bother. I'm all right."

He nodded. "Good-night then. And come again."

She hurried toward the house, wondering if Aunt Gladys knew where she went these afternoons, and if she were watching her even now from her window. She thought of Sexton's passion. I would like to love that way. She thought of love as Sexton had described it, and she wondered what it would be like to be in a man's every waking and sleeping moment. Would he love that way again? Was it possible?

# 5

*R*alph was late on Friday. They held off dinner for him, Aunt Gladys grumbling all the while about how he could have hurried, her whole evening was going to be spoiled, until Iris said, "You go ahead and have your dinner, Aunt Glad. I'll wait and have mine with him."

Aunt Gladys allowed herself to be persuaded.

Iris was glad that they were going to be alone. She wanted it to be the way it always was before Sexton came, she wanted to be glad to see him, to have him there the whole weekend. She would never have said she would marry him unless she felt sure she loved him. It was just a different emotion from the one Sexton had described. Maybe when their lovemaking grew more satisfying everything would change.

But suppose it stayed like this until they were married, suppose even after their marriage it was no more than this. Suppose it was never in their every waking and sleeping moment . . .

She heard the car outside on the drive and ran to the door to open it before he rang, standing on the open threshold and watching him take the steps two at a time as if they were already husband and wife and he were eager to get home to her. He kissed her, and put his arm around her as they went in.

"Sorry, darling. I had some work to finish and got caught up in the evening traffic. How are you? How's my mother?"

He looked in at Aunt Gladys, and ducked out again quickly.

"Can't compete with *The Mortal Coil* or whatever it is she's watching," he grinned.

They sat close together at the long dining table, and she found herself watching him while they ate. He had gray eyes and tow-colored hair that grew low on his forehead. Sometimes she wondered if he modeled himself on Uncle Bill. Bill Tieman had gone to Harvard ages ago, but he still wore a certain cut of jacket and knitted ties, and Ralph did, too. She thought of Sexton with the white dots of paint on his beard, and found herself smiling. Ralph looked at her. She suppressed the smile, before he could ask her why.

Fortunately, at that moment Evans brought in the wine, and Ralph turned to study the bottle. Grandpa had laid down the wine cellar, but Papa hadn't been interested, and she thought sometimes that Ralph knew more about what was down there than anyone else around the place. He always said, "Iris, once we're married I'll go over the wines systematically. Evans has only a vague idea, but I'm sure there are many bottles that have lain too long and should have been used years ago."

Ralph was enchanted with every aspect of the estate. He would manage it expertly once they were married, and there would be no more feathering of anyone's nest. The house would be clean and dusted the way it was when Mama was alive, and the servants would always be on their toes. Whenever Ralph came, they invariably walked about the estate, and he scrutinized everything. He was planning where the putting green would go, and where they should put the swimming pool.

"Funny that your parents never built a pool. Who ever heard of a place this size without a pool?"

She lifted her shoulders. "But they were never here."

"The house looks actually neglected. Wasn't the stonework supposed to be gone over? Look at that long crack under the balcony. Those loose stones need mortar."

"I did write a check for Aunt Gladys. She got an estimate from the masons, and I thought they were going to begin work soon."

"My mother couldn't run her three-room apartment. She probably forgot all about it." He faced her earnestly. "You can't appreciate what it is to live on an estate like this. You have almost an obligation, a trust, to maintain it."

But she had always lived here, and she wasn't as awed by it as Ralph.

After dinner they sat in the inglenook beside the

fireplace, the only private place in the drawing room. The room was a vast sea of sofas and tables and plant stands and Persian rugs and bad paintings, most of them acquired by Grandpa. Even the painting of Mama that reigned over the fireplace was bad, though you could see that Mama was beautiful in spite of the artist, who had made her face too pink, her smile too fixed and her pearls too large. Mama was cream pale, and Iris couldn't imagine her smiling.

Evans remembered that Ralph liked brandy, and brought it to them; Evans was more punctilious about remembering Ralph's tastes than about anyone else's. Over the brandy Ralph told her the news he'd been saving for this moment: he'd been offered a job by an old Boston firm. "I haven't even taken the bar, which means they're pretty confident I'll do okay. Eighteen thousand may not impress you, Iris, but it sure looks like a lot to me. And it's only a start."

"I *am* impressed, Ralph."

He grinned. She had never seen him this excited, even though he was trying hard not to show it.

"It's a beginning. There may be other offers. Hayworth, Stanley and Green. I never thought I'd hear from them."

He hadn't seen her in three weeks. If he were passionately in love, wouldn't he want to touch her, to bring her close? Wouldn't love be more urgent? He caught sight of her watching him, trying to understand him, and maybe he realized he had been remiss, because he drew her against him so that her head rested on his arm.

"I just heard from them this morning, so I'm still trying to take it in. I have been knocking my brains out all these years for just something like this, Iris."

At least it had driven Sexton from his mind. She had been waiting uneasily for him to bring up the matter of Sexton living in the gatehouse, but the job with Hayworth, Stanley and Green had been too much even for that. She felt a great relief when he walked her to her bedroom and said good-night without any mention of Sexton. Still, she knew that sooner or later she would have to explain to Ralph the presence of her new tenant, and she dreaded that coming moment.

The next day they drove out into the country as they usually did while the fine weather lasted. Ralph enjoyed driving her father's sports car. Someone in Boston had told him of a good place to stop for lunch, up the river and then across it into New Hampshire, and so they ended up there. The foliage was at its most brilliant, which brought out a great number of sightseers; the porch of the old inn was thronged, and so was the bar inside. Ralph went in to speak to the hostess, and moments later the hostess called out, "Miss Freebody's table is ready."

Iris was astonished at the speed of the service amid such overcrowding. Ralph must have telephoned for the reservation before they left. On the other hand, he might not have. She did not think he would hesitate to use her name if he thought it would be to any advantage. He wouldn't even understand why she cringed inwardly as they were shown to their table, past the stares of everyone who guessed they had been given preferential treatment. She could almost hear what Ralph would say: "I only told the hostess we would like a table, and the name was Freebody. Why not? It *is* your name."

The gin in her drink finally eased her self-consciousness, and she dared to lift her eyes and look around, at the mountains beyond, at the brown stream running under their window. Why else would anyone marry, unless you wanted it desperately? The thing was to be sure. She mustn't rush into marriage until she was sure—

His voice recalled her. "Iris, what's this about your letting someone live in the gatehouse?"

She sighed. She said, "It's not just like that, Ralph. Dr. Sexton is an assistant professor at the college. Ralph, you know I decided suddenly that I'd try going back to school—"

"My mother wrote me."

"I guess she told you that I . . . that I didn't stay."

"It didn't seem like such a hot idea to me. You're still too shy for all that exposure. And you'd imagine hostility even if it wasn't there."

"Sally Lucas was in my English class. How could I stay? Sexton was the teacher. When I left I forgot my things, and so he brought them to me. And that's how he suggested lessons at home. Ralph, I couldn't think of any good reason to refuse him the gatehouse, since he wanted it so much. I did give it a lot of thought. Maybe it would have been better if I'd said no, but it seemed to me that if the gatehouse were fixed up and someone were living in it, someone who had no connection with what happened . . ."

"Iris. What do you know about the man?"

"The college hired him. They must have checked him."

"But he's going to be part of your household, practically."

"Ralph, you're exaggerating. Just for a few hours a week." She smiled to placate him, but he thought she was making fun of his attitude, and he flushed darkly.

"I don't find it funny, somehow. Have you asked yourself why he took it on himself to return your things? Why he didn't send them over with someone else?"

"Dean Bemis asked him to."

"Why is he so set on living in the gatehouse?"

"He couldn't find a place to live."

"Couldn't find a place to live? In the whole town?"

"That's what he said." Ralph was beginning to sound like a lawyer. She said patiently, "The gatehouse is a lot nicer than any place he'd find, Ralph. It's private, which is what he wanted. And once it's finished . . . Even now, with the walls painted white, and all of Nearing's old junk thrown out—"

"You've seen it? You've been in it with him?"

Her heart beat heavily. "Why not?"

He didn't answer. The luncheon was spoiled. He paid the check glumly, and took her arm and led her out to the car. They started toward home, but he suddenly changed his mind; instead he swerved into a narrow dirt road and parked. Above them yellow and red leaves burned in the sun, casting a hazy radiance.

"Iris, try to understand me. I have to leave you with just my mother and your servants who'd be no damn use at all in an emergency, and I have to be miles away in Boston. Can't you understand why I'm worried about you?"

"I understand, Ralph. But I know I'm quite safe with him."

He took her chin in his hands. "Hell, it's more than that. I am jealous." His gray eyes with their stubby fair lashes looked like the eyes of a lover. He *was* jealous.

"You shouldn't be," she said, putting her hand over his.

He tightened his mouth. "It's all too pat. His getting in to see you, his offering to teach you, his ending up with the gatehouse, and entry to your house. It's happening too fast."

"When you see him, you'll see there's nothing to worry about."

"I'd like to meet him. When we get back?"

She nodded, because she could give no reason for them not to meet.

She had made him happy. He bent over and gave her a light kiss, and then suddenly his arms tightened, and he put his mouth on hers with an insistence she had never felt before. Even his hands moved over her with urgency. This was what she had longed to feel, this was the kind of reassurance she needed that he

*71*

wanted her, this was what would quicken and deepen their relationship, this was the ingredient it had lacked.

Her reaction dismayed her. She felt aloof, and objective, as if she were observing without being part of their embrace.

Panic seized her. I *am* in love with him. I *must* be. She kissed him desperately, as if she could rouse herself with it, but still she felt apart from him for all their straining closeness.

Her simulation of passion had reassured him. When he moved back behind the wheel and started the motor, his voice was his old voice again.

"I've been afraid to rush you, Iris, until I felt you were ready. Maybe I've been wrong."

She didn't answer, and he glanced at her as if surprised that she didn't agree. He backed the car out onto the road and turned toward home.

She heard herself say, "In a way, we're both rushing, Ralph."

"What do you mean? What way?"

She was suddenly frightened, because she was beginning to express a thought she had not fully understood herself. And yet her words went on with a volition of their own. "We're rushing to get married. Why are we? There are so many things ahead of you, adjustments to make, and hard work. You'll want to give your whole mind to studying for the bar, but there'll be the wedding in between, and you know Aunt Glad, she'll want to fuss and make a big production out of it."

72

He frowned.

"And I am thinking seriously of going back to college."

"You can go to college and still be married."

"But all the while things will be happening to both of us! How do we know how we'll feel? How can we be sure how we feel right now about each other, Ralph?"

"I've never had any doubts. I didn't think you did."

Her heart was beating heavily. "I don't. Only. . ." What was she saying? What was she doing? "I just thought, maybe we'd put it off for a few months, till next Christmas maybe, when you can take time off . . ."

His face was pale. "Whose idea is this, Iris? Sexton's?"

It was his inference that she couldn't have ideas of her own that hardened her resistance. "It's my idea, Ralph."

His mouth flattened to a thin line and he began to drive very fast, as if to vent emotions that he did not dare put into words. He said tightly, "Just when everything seemed to be going great—the job, the way you wanted to kiss me. What am I supposed to think now, Iris?"

She was conscience-stricken at his unhappiness. What had impelled her to speak? But in the long run she knew he would come out all right no matter what; he could find any number of girls better-looking than she was, and even rich. Ultimately, indeed, it was she who would be left alone, immured in that great stone house.

Aunt Gladys. Her heart plummeted even further,

thinking of the months ahead, with Aunt Gladys at her heels, questioning, probing, arguing. Aunt Gladys would be prostrated by the delay in their wedding. It had been Aunt Glad's dream from the very moment of Iris's first steps toward recovery. Aunt Glad had watched every move she and Ralph had made toward each other, clocked their awakening interest, known the very moment when he had become the most important factor of her life. Until now.

They were home. He pressed the transmitter in the car and the wrought-iron gates swung wide. They drove through. He parked the car in front of the gatehouse.

Her heart sank. "Should we barge in like this?" The gatehouse door was shut. "Maybe he's busy."

"Then we won't stay. Iris, you did say I could meet him."

Reluctantly she got out of the car with him and rang the bell. The door remained closed. She thought hopefully, maybe he isn't home.

But the door opened, and Sexton stood there in his paint-spattered sweat shirt, frowning and angry, unlike his usual self. His expression cleared a little when he saw them.

She stammered, "I hope you don't mind our coming like this. I wanted you to meet Ralph. Dr. Sexton, Ralph Forsher."

Sexton put out his hand and they shook. The moment lengthened. Why didn't he invite them in?

She stumbled on, "I've been telling Ralph about all

74

the things you've been doing to the gatehouse. I wondered if you . . . if we could. . ."

Sexton seemed to consider, and then he shrugged. "It's not at its best right now. But see for yourself."

Bewildered at his manner, she and Ralph followed Sexton into the living room. Her breath caught in her throat.

The freshly painted white walls were disfigured with an insane arabesque of whorls and curlicues in black paint, laid on with the unmistakable stroke of an aerosol spray can. One wall was covered with giant black letters: GET OUT!

Sexton said grimly, "And then there's this, in case I didn't get the meaning." He led the way into the bedroom. His mattress and box spring were slashed in a dozen places. Hair and cotton wads littered the floor.

Again she caught her breath. It could all be fixed. More paint. New bedding. It was the presence of evil that appalled her, the mindless malevolence, the hate. She managed to say, "Who could have done it? How could they have got in?"

"Kids maybe, through a window," Ralph said. "Maybe even someone from school with a grudge. Anyone can get hold of a spray can. The walls of Boston are covered just like this."

"It's the message that bothers me," Sexton said. "Otherwise I could believe that. The words mean to say something to me."

Ralph said, "What are you thinking of?"

"The obvious. Someone doesn't approve of my being here. This may be the first step in a campaign to frighten me off, or at least make it pretty unpleasant if I stay."

She was absolutely determined to remain calm but, in spite of herself, her legs felt nerveless. She sank down on the nearest chair.

Ralph bent over her, patting her cheeks, chafing her hands. "I think she's going to faint!"

"I'm not," she protested weakly, but Sexton went for brandy anyway and returned with a glass. Ralph held it to her lips.

"I wasn't going to say anything about it," Sexton said. "It happened while I was out this morning, and I planned to clean up the damage before anyone could see it. But when you showed up just now, I was still not thinking clearly, and I couldn't come up with a credible reason to keep you out. Iris, it doesn't involve much. A couple of hours' work and some new bedding, that's all."

"But that someone should feel that way about you, about your living here. That someone should feel that . . . hostile, that he wants to drive you away. . ."

"I'm not going to be scared off that easily. I'm going to find out who did it if only for my own peace of mind. The store in Concord is sending me another mattress and spring, and by tonight the place will be shipshape again. Only this time I keep the doors and windows locked when I'm out, in spite of those electric gates of yours, Iris."

Ralph glanced around. "You've done quite a job

here. You're a handy man with a paintbrush and hammer."

"Come and see the paneling I'm putting up in the kitchen." He led Ralph away.

He said he wouldn't allow himself to be frightened away, but suppose the harassment continued, and suppose it grew worse? Suppose they damaged things he valued, like his stereo, his records, his books? Suppose they . . . attacked him? He would go away. He would have to go away.

Only, she did not want him to go away.

The realization was overwhelming. All the time she had told herself that she had permitted him to come here because he wanted the gatehouse so badly, because he seemed like an interesting man and the conversation in her room had been so strangely comfortable, because he said he wanted to help her with her studies. All this time she had not permitted herself to see the truth. She hadn't even admitted it when she watched for his return the way she watched for Ralph's coming, or when she enjoyed being with him when he worked. It was Sexton who helped her go into the gatehouse again, because she wanted to be with him. It was because of Sexton that she was no longer sure that she wanted to be married. She did not want him to be frightened away. She wanted him to stay.

They were coming back, Ralph and Sexton. She averted her face as if they could read her mind.

"I'd be damned if I'd go to so much trouble to clean up someone else's junk pile," Ralph was saying. "Not unless I planned on staying a long time."

"That depends on Iris," Sexton said. "If she doesn't throw me off the premises, I might stay on indefinitely."

Ralph studied him, considering whether or not he was serious. He said slowly, "I don't know if Iris mentioned it to you, but we had plans to get married in June."

*Had* plans? Not *have* plans? Had Ralph accepted the delay?

"She told me," Sexton said. "Congratulations."

"I only bring it up because the place has been running downhill ever since Iris's parents died. Iris isn't completely able to take over, not yet, and my mother hasn't the foggiest notion about the job. Iris needs more protection. There are people who could still conceivably bear a grudge against the last of the Freebodys. For the mill closing down. For the scandal about the Lucas girl, and Robbie's death. And just because there are crackpots, and villains, and Iris is very rich. There has been one attempt at kidnapping her already."

Sexton stared at him. The silence lengthened. Sexton said levelly, "I assume you have a reason for wanting to scare the daylights out of her."

Ralph flushed, but he said as levelly, "Matter of fact, I do. Iris isn't aware of her danger. Someone should be living in the gatehouse, and patrolling the area. Nearing sits in the kitchen all day drinking coffee, convinced her danger is a thing of the past. Whoever

78

got in and vandalized your house wouldn't have had a chance if the estate was properly guarded."

"True enough," said Sexton.

"Which is why there should be a gatekeeper in the gatehouse."

She did not dare look at Sexton. "Ralph, I told Dr. Sexton that he could stay here this year."

"And he should, since he's already gone to this much trouble to make the place livable. I'm only thinking of the future, when he leaves. When—if—we're married."

"Of course, I might apply for the position of gate-keeper," Sexton said gravely. "The job is very attractive, coming with a nice place to live."

Ralph didn't seem to know whether or not to laugh. "You're kidding."

"Not entirely. Living here is damned comfortable, and cheap. I might quit teaching for a while and get back on a book I started. Being a gatekeeper isn't half as demanding a job as teaching. I'm handy, as you can see, and I learned how to shoot in the army."

Ralph decided to laugh. "We'll think it over," he said. "Iris, let's let Dr. Sexton get back to work. And he has plenty."

Sexton walked them to their car and saw them drive away. Ralph said almost at once, "Looks to me as if he were digging in for a long stay."

"It was only for the year. That was understood."

"I'd rather be too careful than not careful enough where you're concerned, Iris. And I have a hunch he's covering something. Burying himself out in the country. Why should anyone who taught at Columbia be ready to settle for a job in a hick college like Freebody?"

"I think he did want to get away from New York. His wife was killed—"

"Killed?" he said sharply. "How?"

"An accident. He didn't say. Ralph, who could have done that to the gatehouse?" She wanted to get the talk away from Dr. Sexton.

"I still think it was kids. Someone who could shinny in over a wall and sneak through a window."

*Unless that someone were on the premises to begin with.* She blocked the thought out of her mind.

He swerved to a stop in front of the house. "Do you want to drive to Concord tonight to see a movie?"

"I'd love it."

She left him with the car, examining the motor, and ran upstairs. The house enshrouded her, dark and cold, after the bright outdoors. She felt oppressed and ill at ease, as if something bad had happened. She started, but it was only Coffey coming out of the shadows.

"You all right, love?"

"Fine, Coffey. I didn't see you, that's all."

"You look worried. Did he say something to get you upset?"

"No! I'm just hurrying to have a bath before dinner."

"That Sally Lucas was here. Second time this week."

Iris stopped dead. "Sally Lucas? Here?"

"Comes to see Nearing. Real sudden, her getting

next to Nearing. Unless she figures he has money stashed away. Fat chance he'd leave it to her!"

Nearing had never forgiven Sally for having aborted Robbie's baby, his only hope of a child of his blood. Sally getting next to Nearing? Why? The money? Or could it be a way of obtaining entry onto the estate? Sally must know about Dr. Sexton living in the gatehouse. Everyone knew how strictly she had always kept to herself; the whole town must be talking about how the wrought-iron gates had flown open for Sexton. Would Sally want to drive him away, to get back at her?

All through dinner, Aunt Gladys kept looking from Ralph to Iris, surmising something in their silence. Ralph was as glad to get away from the house as she was. He remained preoccupied throughout the ride to Concord, and even in the movie he seemed fidgety and restless. When she suggested he might like to leave before the end, he protested, so they stayed to the finish, he doggedly pretending he was interested, she sunk in remorse.

When he left on Sunday it was without any further reference to their postponed wedding plans. His kiss was perfunctory, and he looked unhappy. When she called after him, "When will I see you again?" he said, "I'm not sure. I'll let you know."

She turned back into the house, a lump in her throat, to find Aunt Gladys standing in the hall, shaking her head at her.

"Iris. Iris. You foolish girl."

Aunt Gladys had guessed something was wrong, and then badgered Ralph until he told her.

"Aunt Glad, I don't think waiting awhile to get married is foolish, if that's what you're thinking of. He has so many things to think about now—graduation, the bar exams, the job . . ."

"Iris, you're letting that man influence you."

"He doesn't even know I've asked Ralph to wait."

"Iris, he wants to come between you and Ralph."

"If Ralph and I are in love, no one and nothing can come between us."

Aunt Gladys's laugh was bitter. "Who told you that fairy tale? Coffey? You tell a man like Ralph with a face a little like Robert Redford, same kind of hair and eyes, that you're in no hurry to get married and he'll find himself a girl who wants him too much to wait. Plenty of pretty girls in Boston. With money, too. You can't play games with Dr. Sexton and not have Ralph do the same thing in Boston."

"I'm not playing games with anyone, Aunt Glad." Iris had to walk around her to reach the stairs.

"Iris, just listen to me a minute. You don't have your poor mother to tell you what's what, and it would kill me to see you get hurt again. A fine young man is in love with you. You love him. Or you did until that man came. Don't take a chance on losing him, Iris. That man has wormed his way into your house and now into your heart. He has you eating out of his hand."

She continued to mount the stairs. "Aunt Glad, I do like Dr. Sexton, and I hope he likes me. But he's only my teacher, and someone living in our gatehouse. If I don't want to rush into marriage, it isn't because of him—"

"Iris, you fool!" The words were propelled from Aunt Gladys's mouth with all the force of her exasperation. She caught herself, color mottled her florid cheeks, and her hand went to her heart. "I shouldn't have said that. You have me so worked up I don't know what I'm saying. I'm not so smart either, but I know men, and I can't stand to see you fall for that schemer."

"Aunt Gladys."

Aunt Gladys fell silent at the tone in her voice.

"I appreciate your worrying about me, and your advice. But please, from now on, don't interfere."

She continued up the stairs, but not before she had caught a glimpse of Aunt Gladys's face. She had expected to see dismay and disbelief at this unfamiliar show of firmness—even anger. What she was not prepared for was the look of pure panic in Aunt Gladys's expression.

# 6

Sally Lucas stopped at his desk on her way out after class.

"You going home after school tonight, Dr. Sexton?"

"Yes. I may be a little late."

"You always tear out of here at four."

He grinned. Was that the way it looked? "I've been trying to get my house ready before the bad weather. It's practically finished now. Why do you want to know?"

"I was hoping I could get a lift with you to the Castle. My car is being fixed, and I told Mr. Nearing I'd be out there this evening and I don't want to disappoint him. He makes us dinner when I come."

He found himself hesitating. If he didn't take her, she'd find other means, and besides, how could he decently refuse? Because she had frightened Iris away? It would take very little to frighten Iris. "I've been meaning to stay on and take care of some records," he said slowly. "I'm not sure exactly when I'll leave—"

"Just don't go without me, please?" she said, and smiled pleadingly. "I'll watch for you from the Student Union. I can see where your car is parked from there."

It was later than he expected when he finished work, locked the office and went out toward his car. Sally had slipped his mind, but now he saw her running across the parking area, clutching her books. In her short skirt and long black stockings, a plaid tam over her hair, she had a rather charming, *gamine* look. He came around to open the door for her, but she quickly let herself in.

Each day, it seemed, was colder than the last. A raw wind blew the last of the leaves from the trees and sent them scudding dryly across his windshield as they drove away from town.

She shivered. "I hate the winters here."

"I'm surprised you didn't pick a college in the South, then, where the winters are milder. Schools in the South are often less expensive."

"I live with my sister here, so it doesn't cost much, and I work nights at the café to help see me through." Her glance was sidelong. "Trying to get me out of town, Doc?"

He was too astonished to protest, and before he got his chance to, she said, "You know a lot more about me than you did that first day. *She* told you about me, didn't she?"

He was careful. "I've heard stories. From different sources. This is a small community. People talk."

"Then you know about the baby." He was silent, and she said, "Iris got sick about it, and didn't want the

85

baby destroyed. Neither did Nearing. He wanted
Robbie's baby, and he went to Iris's father. Her father
thought it would help Iris if he gave me the money. So
the Freebodys gave me five thousand to have it. But
how could I have a baby on just five thousand? How
long could I last, with a baby? And why should they
think they could tell me how to live my life for a
measly five thousand?"

Her look was angry.

"She was embarrassed when I showed up in your
class, wasn't she? I know she must have left because of
me."

"Sally, the Freebodys had nothing to do with your
getting pregnant. They gave you the money out of
kindness, if you can bring yourself to admit it. They
weren't obligated to you."

She gave a half smile. "You're on her side already.
Not that I blame you. You live on her estate, why
shouldn't you be grateful? But Iris knows she could
have got the money for Robbie, and he wouldn't have
had to kill himself. She was angry and she was jealous,
and so she didn't get the money."

"I think she would have got the money for Robbie if
she could. She tried every way she knew."

"And you believe her rather than me. You take her
side because she's rich and important. And you'd like
to see me get out of town because she wants that. Go
to a school in the South. Get lost. Disappear, so as not
to embarrass Iris Freebody anymore."

"That's not fair, Sally. I only brought up the south-
ern school because you complained about the winter.

Why should it matter to me where you go to school? Anyway," he said, because they were skirting the long wall of Adam's Castle and he wanted to leave her on a more positive note, "it's all water under the bridge by now, and time to forget it. She was a kid of sixteen when it happened."

"So? I was fourteen. Old enough to get pregnant. You're taking her side, that's all. I'll bet she's real nice to you. She must be pretty darn happy to have you there. Who does she get to talk to in that mausoleum? Only the fellow she's engaged to, and he's never around. The whole town knows he's marrying her for her money. Who'd look at her twice if she wasn't rich and a Freebody? Even Robbie wouldn't touch her when he wanted sex, and that's why she couldn't forgive him."

They had given him a transmitter for his car so he could come and go freely. The gates opened for him. He headed up the drive. "I'll drop you off at Nearing's."

He must have sounded short, because she turned her head. "Are you sore at me? Because I talked about her that way?" When he didn't answer she said, "You *are* sore, I can tell. You like her, don't you?"

"Here's where you get off," he said, swinging around at the garage where Nearing had his rooms on the floor above.

"You really like her? I just can't believe it," she said, her eyes widening.

"Sally, I'm in a hurry."

She opened the door and got out, pressing her books

against her chest, her pretty face mocking. "You can do better, Doc. Without looking too far, either. Thanks for the lift."

He swung back toward the gatehouse, irritated, amused, and yet disturbed. The car held her presence, an indefinable fragrance. Sexy, all right. No wonder Robbie lost his head.

Tonight he was giving Iris a lesson. They had started last week, and a pattern was forming to his days. He found himself looking forward to his evenings at the Castle just as he knew she looked forward to them. She was always at the door when he rang the bell, opening it herself, drawing him in. Sometimes he had the feeling that she reached out for him like a drowning swimmer seizing a lifeline.

He opened the door to the gatehouse. Almost finished. It still lacked furniture, but the shelves were up and stained and his books were on them, and the stereo was working fine. He had found an old set of wicker porch furniture in a secondhand shop in town and carried it home with him and painted it yellow and put it in the kitchen. He changed into his flannel shirt and sneakers and went into the kitchen to broil a steak and fix a salad. The hi-fi was playing Berlioz, sweeping, drenched with emotion. He ate, and read his paper, and felt a surge of feeling that was like happiness. He hadn't believed it possible that Frannie would ever be exorcised, that happiness would be his again, if even for brief soaring moments like these. He wondered if it was only living in the gatehouse that filled him with well-being, or was it more. Was it the evening ahead with Iris Freebody? He stopped, surprised. It must have been Sally Lucas who put that notion in his head.

He washed up neatly, turned off the music and with the theme still singing inside him, he walked up to the Castle.

Iris was waiting. It seemed to him that each time he came she would let out her breath in a faint sigh when she saw him, as if she had not been sure he would show up. She led him upstairs to her room and shut the door, as she had that first time. The lamps were lit, and there was a fire in the hearth which flickered with a red luster on the mahogany paneling. He smiled. "Cozy," he said, settling himself into his chair.

"Do you think so? You said this room was too heavy and dark for me, so I had Evans take off the velvet drapes."

"The fire makes a difference, too. I didn't see the room with the fire lit before."

"I never bothered with it before. It *is* cheerful, isn't it?" The uncertain look vanished, and she gave another sigh, of relief and pleasure.

He opened his book, but almost at once she interrupted. "I did mean to ask you. We have acres of furniture in our attic. Would you like any of it for your house? It's dreadful stuff, most of it, but good, and my mother had it put up there because there simply wasn't room for all of it."

"That would be great. If you're sure it's all right."

"It's mine. Why shouldn't it be all right?" She hesitated. "You can come up now and look at it, if you want."

He put down his book and followed her, up the stairs to a hall like the one below, only more drab, with plain doors set in plaster walls. One of the doors was partially opened, and he could see a light through the opening. Why did he think someone stood behind the door, watching them, listening?

"This is the servants' floor," she said. They climbed on, still higher, and came to a door set at the top of the steps. She opened it and pressed a switch.

Furniture, trunks, boxes, rolled rugs, statuary in bronze and white marble, bicycles, dress forms . . . He smiled, and she did, too.

"Do you think there's anything? I mean, it *is* pretty awful, isn't it? Grandpa toured Europe once and brought everything back he thought looked grand."

"Now there's an interesting piece. I could use it in the living room." It was oak, Jacobean, he thought, with a big lid that let down and would make a fine writing surface, and plenty of cubbyholes behind it. "Of course, if it's valuable—"

"I'll have Nearing pick it up and take it over for you tomorrow. This chair is very comfortable. When I was little, I'd hide up here sometimes and read in it."

"That's good enough reason," he said. "Could I have it, too?"

He picked out another table, and another chair, and then they returned downstairs to her room. Again he had the feeling that someone had listened, someone had watched their progress.

"All the servants sleep up there?"

"All except Nearing and Wolfe, our chauffeur. But they all stay downstairs in their own sitting room, mostly. Only Coffey stays in her room."

So it must have been Coffey listening, guarding the child she had raised. If she looked like a witch, it was a good witch who dabbled only in protective spells.

"You have an odd household," he said. "Is anyone under sixty?"

She smiled. "They've all been here forever. Except Nearing, and he came when I was still a baby." She paused. "Maybe they are old, and not very efficient, but I like them and they like me, I think. And I trust them."

"That's what matters."

She paused again, a little longer this time. "Aunt Gladys . . . well, she's difficult to live with, but I'm sure she only wants me to be happy."

"I have a feeling she isn't fond of me," he said.

She didn't answer.

"I don't know what I've done to offend her," he continued, "except live in the gatehouse."

Color surged up into her face. "You see, she thinks you have an influence on me."

He was astounded. "She does? I do?"

Her color deepened. "I told Ralph when he was here that I thought we should wait a little before getting married, like another six months, maybe. My aunt blames you."

"Blames me?" He could only echo her words in his astonishment. "But we never even talked about it—yes, we did, but all I said was that you should be sure. I'm sure she'd want you to be sure, if she's interested in your happiness. And her stepson's. She couldn't quarrel with that."

"You made me question myself, and my feelings," Iris said. "Sometimes it seems to me that all my life people have always given me a little push and said, 'Go there, that's best for you.' And I've gone where they told me. This is the first time I ever asked myself why."

"I don't want to be the cause of any grief."

"No. I'm glad you said what you did. It made me think about myself, and what I wanted, for the first time."

It was he now who was at a loss for words. There was something intensely intimate in what she had said, and what she had left unsaid, and he was disconcerted. To cover his confusion he opened the textbook.

"How far have you read?"

They settled down, and were well into Chaucer before he stretched, and looked at his watch.

"Ten-thirty. Time to quit."

She was disappointed. She said eagerly, "I'm not at all tired."

"I am," he said. "It's been a long day for Chaucer."

When they went downstairs, the sitting-room door was open, and the aunt stood up when she saw them. "Working late, Dr. Sexton," she said coldly. "You're very generous with your time."

"Time flies when you enjoy your work," he said

imperturbably. "Good-night, Mrs. Forsher. Good-night, Iris."

"I'll send Nearing over tomorrow with the furniture."

He hesitated. "If it's at all possible, could Nearing wait with it until I get home? I've been keeping the place locked up since it was broken into, and I'd rather be home when he brings everything."

' "I'll tell Nearing to watch for you."

When he came home the next day, he had hardly let himself in and done the quick check he now found himself doing, with beating heart, wondering if he would find everything as he'd left it, when Nearing rang his bell and the estate truck backed up to the door.

He helped Nearing with the heavy pieces, and while he was pushing them into place, Nearing came back with a roll of carpets. He untied them and spread them out. They were Persian, threadbare but still handsome.

"Miss Freebody says you're welcome to them, if you can use them."

"They're magnificent."

Nearing was glancing around. "This is a bad house, no matter how you cover it up."

It was the first time the thought came to him: It could have been Nearing who scrawled on his walls and slashed his mattress, not so much venting his hate on him as on the house.

"It's damned comfortable if you haven't a place to live."

"You sure wanted it bad enough," Nearing said. "I remember you that first time, climbing onto the gate to get a better look at it. You'd have been smarter to find yourself a place in town. This is a bad-luck house."

"Maybe the bad luck has run out by now."

"Some people have queer tastes," Nearing said. "You couldn't get me to stay a night in a house where a child hung himself."

He thanked Nearing for his help, and when he showed him out he wondered about a second latch on the door. No telling if Nearing might get tanked up on beer one day and come back and hack the house to bits.

He waited to thank Iris until the next night, when he was due to give her another lesson.

She was pleased by his appreciation. "Do they really look good?" she said, about the carpets.

"Perfect. It's just the touch the place needed. You'll have to come and see for yourself."

"Later?"

He hesitated. "As a matter of fact, I'm going back to school later. They're showing a French film I wanted to see, at nine in the Language Hall, and I was planning to make this a short lesson."

She didn't say anything, but when he closed his book after an hour, again she looked disappointed. On the spur of the moment he said, "Why don't you come with me? It's supposed to be very good, took first prize at the Cannes festival."

Her face lit up briefly, and then was extinguished. "I couldn't."

"Sally Lucas again? I hardly think she'll turn up there. Besides, she works nights. I dropped her here one afternoon and she told me she has a job."

"You dropped her here?"

He was uncomfortable. "She asked me for a lift. Her car broke down. Look, Iris, no one will notice you. We'll be late getting there and the lights will be out, and if it's important to you we can sneak off before the lights go on again."

He could tell she wanted to go. He said, "You're feeling all this new independence. Don't stop now. Don't start being afraid again."

She said slowly. "Well—if you don't mind waiting. I'll only be a minute."

She vanished into her bedroom. He was not unmindful of the fact that the real reason she was going might be not to see the film but to be with him. It must be because she was so starved for company, to be with someone a little nearer her own age. If Ralph were here more often, it would be different. So he told himself, as he ruled out any other possibility that might lead to uncharted land where he was afraid to venture.

Mrs. Forsher was waiting for them at her sitting-room door as they went past.

"Iris, are you going out?"

"Just to see a movie on campus. I won't be late."

The aunt's eyes raked him. "Take good care of her, Dr. Sexton."

There was hatred in her voice. It shocked him. He tried to answer lightly. "I'll return her in the same condition I found her." The aunt did not think it amusing, nor did he. An incredible thought came to him. The aunt was capable of taking a knife to his mattress, of scrawling on his walls. She would have to be slightly mad, but who wanted him out more?

They walked down the driveway to where his car was parked.

"Did I say your aunt wasn't exactly fond of me? I'll revise that. She dislikes me intensely."

In the light of the dashboard he could see Iris's face as he helped her inside. She was sucking on her lower lip. "It's because of me, mainly," she said.

"How?"

She took a long time answering. "She's afraid I may like you."

Again he was disconcerted. He was more used to talking with women in the half-sincere, half-bantering dialogue that usually went with sexual awareness. He said, "*Do* you like me?"

She said quietly, "Yes, I do."

He started the motor, and they drove through the opened gates while he tried to think what to say. Adam's Castle had been an impregnable citadel to him when he first saw it, and yet the gatehouse had fallen to him without a struggle. Iris he was handling warily, as if she were a bird that had dropped into his cupped hands and must be nursed gingerly. And yet she showed no distrust or alarm and seemed perfectly content to rest there. His taste in women ran to soft, boneless types, like Frannie, in whom he had never suspected that calculating nature or a spine of ice. Iris now, with her long legs folded up inside the tweed tent she wore, her straight hair like a horse's mane tangled on her collar, her strong fingers without jewelry, without even gloves, clasped together in the tension of the moment, was not the kind of female for whom he'd ever felt a sexual attraction. If he ever wanted a woman again, and sometimes he wondered if the emotion was possible for him now, it would more likely be someone like Sally Lucas he would turn to than Iris Freebody. He could take Sally without having to think, or look backward. It could never be that way with Iris.

"I guess I shouldn't have told you," she said.

"No. No. Why shouldn't you have, if it's true. I like you, too, Iris. These evenings with you, I find I look forward to them."

"You do, really?" She was astonished.

He parked the car and led her around through the back door of the Language Hall and in the darkness managed to find two empty seats in a back row. Concentration was difficult. A girl in the film was murdered by her lover. . . . His thoughts went back to Frannie, burned to death. *Do you like me? Yes, I do. I like you, too.* The words were part of another life, as clean and simple as the Vermont air outside. He repeated them to help desperately until he rid his mind of the picture of Frannie's burned body.

They saw the last of the movie standing behind the last row, while he helped Iris into her coat, and they were in their car and moving out even before the first of the other moviegoers reached the parking lot.

"Would you like to stop for a drink? I know a pleasant bar on the highway patronized by locals. No college students."

"Someone might . . . recognize me. And you."

"An ice-cream soda? We can drive into some other town."

"I don't like to spoil your evening, but . . ." She shook her head.

"Tell you what," he said, "you come back with me to the gatehouse and I'll show you how the furniture looks, and we'll have some Calvados. Put a French finish on the evening."

"Calvados?"

"Apple brandy. A friend brought me a bottle from Normandy."

She agreed. They drove home and he parked his car alongside the house and led her through crunching leaves to his yellow door.

Inside, she exclaimed with pleasure. The rugs were just right; they added color to the white room. And the Jacobean desk looked like something out of a museum.

"Save your compliments till I light the fire." It didn't take long; there were dried pieces from the night before, and he rolled his old newspapers into spills which he kept in a basket.

She had settled into the deep chair comfortably, as well she might, since it had been hers long before it was his.

"I'll get the Calvados," he said. There was no place

to put the bottle and the glasses, and the cheese and crackers, so he had to set the tray on the floor in front of the fire. But she left her chair and joined him beside the tray.

"How could you tell when you first saw the gate-house that it would turn out so beautifully?" she said.

"It looked as if the frame was sound. Broken windows and doors aren't important. You see, we bought this derelict brownstone in Brooklyn, and we transformed it. And I did a good deal of the carpentry and wiring myself."

She sipped the Calvados, gasped, and laughed.

"It's strong stuff. Better have a cracker with it," he advised.

"It's lovely," she said. "I think I can actually smell the apples. About the gatehouse. I meant, what made you come and look at it? Did anyone tell you about it? Or me?"

"It was sheer chance. I'd heard about Old Adam's Castle, of course, but I honestly didn't know there would be a gatehouse, or that you would be nice enough to let me live in it." She wanted to believe him, he could see that; she was fighting any doubts that lingered. "What reason did you think I might have had?" he said gently.

"Oh, no! None! I mean, I just wondered!" She had another drink. "I do smell apples. I've never been to Normandy. Have you? I'd like to travel, sometime."

"I was in France while I was still going to college. One summer. It wasn't long enough, one summer, but I didn't have any money to stay longer even if I'd had

99

the time. What's preventing you from travel, if it's what you want?"

"I wouldn't go *alone!*" She looked aghast at the idea.

"You'll be going on a honeymoon soon."

"Ralph wants to go to the West Coast."

"But what about you? Do you want to go to the West Coast?"

She smiled. "I . . . never thought of it that way, I mean, if Ralph—well, I don't mind going to the West Coast. There'll be other times, and then we'll go where I want, too."

"Sure you will," he said. "My money's on you. You're making great strides."

"When you were in France, did you go to Normandy?"

"I spent a week in a small place called Honfleur on the sea. It's probably all motels by now and overrun by tourists, but when I was there it was cobbled streets and half-timbered houses no higher than your eyebrows. And a gray stone harbor coming right up into the main square, so that the masts of a hundred fishing boats stood right there up against the buildings."

"If I ever get to France I'll make a point of going there," she said. Her face was suffused with warmth, the heat of the fire, the brandy . . . Did he have anything to do with it? He thought of the bird in his palm that seemed content to stay. "I think I'm getting drunk," she said. "The walls are tumbling down. I'm twenty-one, and I don't have to answer to anyone."

"Good," he said. "And now maybe I'd better take

you home, before you drink any more. This is the time to stop, while you're feeling this way."

"I don't want to stop. I want to stay here. I hate the Castle. I like it here, with you."

He was uneasy now. It was happening too fast, whatever was happening, and he wasn't ready to take on any emotional entanglements; he was still too deeply enmeshed in his own. He didn't want to hurt her, and she might be the kind of girl who would fly into the face of things, and be as wrong about him as she was about Ralph.

"Come along, Iris," he said. "I promised your aunt I would take care of you, and what will she think if she sees you staggering up the stairs and smelling of apples?"

"I'm not getting drunk that way," she said. "I just feel good, and free. I won't stagger."

"Let's see if you do." He pulled her to her feet and put her into her coat. He led her outside, considered driving her to the house, and then decided to walk. The walk and the cold air might clear her head.

He said, "Next time we'll be more wary about the Calvados."

"Please don't be. Whatever it is, I think it's the first time in my life I've ever been happy."

He put his arm through hers so as not to imply too indelicately that she might need support. The rhododendron leaves had curled up into thin spindles against the cold, and he could still smell the smoke from his fire spicing the air. He gulped deeply, and his nostrils shrank.

"I've never spent a winter in Vermont. Is it very bad?"

"It snows. And the snow stays. You'll like it, Dr. Sexton."

"Ian."

"Ian. You mustn't go away because of the snow. Or anybody."

"I have no intention of going away. I'm going to wax my skis and go skiing. Will you come with me?"

"Oh, yes. We have hills on the estate, where I used to ski with Robbie."

"All the marvelous runs, and you stay on the estate? I'll have to show you places closer than Honfleur that you'll enjoy."

She laughed with pleasure, her face close to his. He had the feeling she wanted him to kiss her, and yet he held back, afraid. I don't want to hurt her. I'm not sure I'm ready. One thing about a tall girl, her mouth was very close and you didn't have to bend down, like with Frannie. Frannie's smoke-blackened face hung between them, and vanished in an instant. He breathed again. The brandy had got to him, too. He touched her cold cheeks with his hand.

"I hope I haven't been stupid," she said. "The Calvados was very strong, and maybe I said things I shouldn't have."

"You were just fine," he said. "Feeling better?"

"Yes. But I felt good before."

"We'll do it again. Let's see, next Tuesday, right?"

She nodded.

"Damn," he said. "My briefcase. I left it in your room."

"Come up with me and get it."

"What will your aunt say if she sees me?"

"She's asleep. And anyway, she has no right to say anything, does she?"

"No, she doesn't." He smiled. "But let's try not to wake her, anyway."

She unlocked the door with care. There was only a small night light burning—because of the energy crisis, she whispered to him—and they tiptoed across the hall and up the stairs without a sound. She opened the door to her room, and shut it again before she switched on the light.

He felt the cold in the room at once, and noticed that the draperies were blowing. "You must have left a window open," he said.

"It isn't a window. It's the balcony door."

"I didn't know you had a balcony in your room. Is it the kind you can stand out on?"

She nodded. "Come and look. I can see the roof of the gatehouse from it, now that there aren't any leaves."

Did she look down at the gatehouse often? Was it because he lived in it? He went to join her on the balcony, picking up his briefcase as he went, from where it lay at the foot of the chair.

"You have to lean out a little," she said. "Then you can look down almost to the gates."

He leaned out beside her. The night sparkled with frost, and the mountains were black—

Under their hands a segment of stone balustrade disappeared. He stared dumbfounded for that split second before the pieces of stone crashed and splintered on the stone terrace below. Then, acting without thought, he seized her and dragged her back just as the concrete beneath their feet gave way. He leaned against the doorjamb and stared at the sagging steel rods projecting into nothingness where the floor had been.

She was trembling. He put his arm around her and held her, and she let her face rest against his coat.

It was only moments later that a door opened in the far hall, and someone ran down to the bedroom and opened the door.

"Iris!"

It was Mrs. Forsher, her face gray, her gold hair loose on the collar of a satin robe. She put out a hand to the nearest chair back for support. "Oh, my God, you're all right," she gasped. "I heard the crash from my room, and the first thing I thought of was the balcony, and how you like to stand on it at night."

Iris moved away from him. "We could have been killed," she said inaudibly.

"Oh, my God," said the aunt again. "And it's all my fault. I meant to call the masons in. They gave me an estimate, and you even gave me a check for them, but somehow it slipped my mind. All this upset lately, I—"

"You could have been killed."

It was Coffey saying it this time. She leaned on her cane, her bad leg twisted, her wrapper undone, her eyes burning with anger.

It was the sight of Coffey that seemed to calm Iris, or made her at least pretend to calmness for Coffey's sake.

104

"I wasn't killed. It was just an accident. Why doesn't everybody go to bed?" Her voice rose a little, and began to tremble again.

"It's her fault," Coffey said, pointing to Mrs. Forsher. "Don't let her tell you it slipped her mind. She was hoping and waiting for the balcony to fall."

"You crazy fool!" the aunt cried. "You're a lunatic! If it were up to me, you'd have been in a lunatic asylum long ago!"

"Iris! Iris!" came Coffey's outraged plea.

He glanced at Iris's white face, and moved in. "Let's let Iris get to bed. This can wait till morning. She's had a shock, and the best thing is a night's sleep."

"Iris," Coffey said, disregarding him, "don't let her fool you! From the minute she set foot in this house I knew she was going to make it hers, lock, stock and barrel! She and that stepson—"

He took Coffey's arm firmly. "Let me help you upstairs, Miss Coffey."

She stared at him as though she had not seen him before. "What are you doing here?"

"I brought Iris home from the movies," he said.

She seemed suddenly quieted, and he was able to lead her out and up to her room.

At her door she turned and looked at him from under shaggy gray brows. "What do you want with her? You after her money, too?"

"I'm her friend," he said. "I think she needs friends right now."

Her glance searched, and appraised. "She's in danger of her life, do you know that? The balcony is

105

just the beginning, mark my words. That aunt of hers would like to see her dead."

"Why should she want Iris dead, Miss Coffey?" He hoped his quiet voice would continue to calm her. "Her stepson is going to marry Iris, and she wants that very much."

"Suppose they don't get married?" The eyes looked at him with startling shrewdness. She drew him inside her room and shut the door. Her voice was a harsh, broken whisper. "Did Iris tell you her aunt and Ralph would inherit everything if she were to die now, before she got married?"

"No, she didn't," he said. His mouth was dry.

"Her mother was mad at her own side of the family for looking down their noses at Iris's father and thinking him common, and she made it part of her will that they were never to get anything. The money was Iris's father's only while he was alive, in trust for Iris. The only relatives left that were never specifically disinherited were Mrs. Forsher and Ralph. If Iris dies, or gets killed, and she isn't married and doesn't have children of her own, the money is all theirs."

He could say only, "But she *is* marrying Ralph."

Coffey's mouth twisted. "They're scared, don't you see? That aunt of hers is wise enough in her own interests. She knows Iris likes you. She was afraid of that from the beginning. Why do you think she never wanted you here?"

"Iris may like me—I hope she does—but she's marrying Ralph. They only postponed the wedding a few months."

"That's not what Mrs. Forsher thinks. You should

have heard the goings-on when she found out the wedding was put off. I heard her screaming at Ralph, and him screaming back. She gave him a time. I was almost sorry for him. Mrs. Forsher is scared out of her wits that there'll never be a wedding and all she'll be left with is the income they gave her. She had something to do with that balcony tonight. She's in and out of Iris's room when Iris is with you. She was there tonight."

He thought of the balcony door left open. It had been closed when he and Iris left, or they would have been aware of the cold.

Coffey was saying, "Maybe she let the stonework go, hoping something like this would happen. And maybe she helped it along. She's scared enough to do something batty, and she isn't that smart to begin with, except where it comes to herself."

The aunt had been near hysteria tonight; she couldn't have simulated that, or the gray pallor of her face. But was she hysterical because Iris had nearly been killed, or because she hadn't been? The aunt was a cold customer, and he doubted she had any love for Iris. If she had, would she have tried so hard to keep her sequestered? Would she have fed Iris's fears of the world outside?

"She's been in the gatehouse, too. Nearing still has a key hanging in the pantry. I don't know what she did there, but she was in it all right. I saw her walk down there, and she took her time coming back."

So it might have been the aunt who vandalized the gatehouse.

"If you're her friend, Dr. Sexton, keep an eye on her.

I wish I could protect her more, but I'm not much good for anything now."

"You're doing fine," he said. "Good-night, Miss Coffey."

He left her and went downstairs.

Iris was waiting. She looked at him somberly. "There were cracks in the balcony for the longest time. And the balustrade was shaky, I could feel it. Ian, it was just an accident, wasn't it?"

"Sure, that's probably all it was. There was the weight of the two of us on it, which was an additional strain, and the cracks might have been pretty deep after last winter." He wasn't going to frighten her any more tonight, though eventually she would have to be made aware of her danger, if she *was* in danger. "Iris, when you call the masons in—and you should at once—would you have them come at a time when I can be here with them?" He wanted to see their reactions firsthand and on the spot, to see if they thought it was only the stresses of ice and time and age that had weakened and collapsed the balcony, or if something, or someone, could have helped it along.

She said she would arrange it. "If it wasn't an accident," she said slowly, "then someone must hate me very much."

He put his hands on her shoulders and propelled her back into her room. "Whatever happened, we were damned lucky. Think of it that way for tonight. Go to sleep, Iris. You need that. I'll see you tomorrow, if I may."

He retrieved his briefcase again and let himself out.

As he walked down the driveway he had a fleeting memory of the magic of the evening, and in its way it *had* been magical, strangely so, in spite of all the other factors. He thought of Coffey's words, unfounded and irrational, maybe, but ominous enough to strengthen his own suspicions. What to do? He was too tired and shaken himself to think clearly, except for the one clear, luminous certainty: what happened to Iris Freebody had become all at once very important to him.

# 7

*T*here was a note pushed through the mail slot in his door when he came home the next night. It was from Iris; she had arranged with the masons to check the balcony on Saturday, when he was home. Would he be able to make it at eleven?

He waited for the Ideal Stucco and Concrete Company truck to enter the gates before he followed it to the house on Saturday. It might be embarrassing to Iris if her aunt questioned her about his presence, and he hoped he might get lost in the activity. But the sitting-room door was open when Iris let him in, and Mrs. Forsher's head turned toward him briefly and then away without an attempt at even a formal nod.

"Dr. Sexton was on the balcony with me when it collapsed," Iris said clearly to the two men who waited with her in the hall. "So he's especially interested in what happened." Plainly, she hoped her words would carry to the sitting room, but Mrs. Forsher's face remained averted.

He crouched with the two masons at the edge of what remained of the balcony, while they examined it.

"Hard to tell," one of them said. "If there was a crack, and ice got in, and expanded. . ."

"House like this wasn't meant to have balconies," the other said. "Looks as if they changed their minds and added them midway. That might make them weak."

He pointed to places where the mortar stopped cleanly. The mason shook his head. "It could have fallen out when the break happened. I've seen it like that. The best thing is not to worry about how it happened, but fix it up good and strong. I warned the other lady, Mrs. Forsher, that there were places where the stonework might give way, especially when the frost set in, but she never did get around to giving me the go-ahead, and I had jobs piling up before the bad weather, so I didn't remind her. But I did warn her about this balcony."

Iris must have been listening while they talked. When they stepped back he saw her there, her face withdrawn.

The masons would start on Monday. They left, and he remained behind with Iris, staring through the open French doors as the masons' truck circled and went down the driveway.

"Ian, I know what you're thinking. Coffey thinks so, too. She spoke to me. But there's no proof, is there?"

"None." Except that the aunt knew of the danger and had done nothing about it; knew there would be months ahead and she could wait and take her time, and one of those days Iris would step out on her balcony and lean out, looking toward the gatehouse, maybe . . . "But she was criminally careless."

"Yes, but Aunt Glad is like that. She lives in a world of fiction, other people's lives, that she watches on TV. She isn't bad, Ian, just—well, not too bright. She came and lived here when I needed her, when there was no one else. I know she wouldn't hurt me, Ian, not deliberately."

What could he say? That Mrs. Forsher, soft and plump and pretending love, could be as hard as Frannie underneath? Harder, because Frannie had something to look forward to; she had been young and beautiful and could anticipate men and success and even money. But Mrs. Forsher had nothing but Iris, and if she thought she would lose her, too, the wheels in her head might go haywire, and do what they weren't programed for. And I'm the monkey wrench in the machinery, he thought. I'll be the one to drive her to hurt Iris.

He went back to his house and tried to enjoy puttering around, arranging his shelves, bringing down some spare outlets. But his mind was bothered. She isn't even the kind of girl I'm attracted to, he thought. He liked the smell of perfume, and silken legs and high heels, all the excitement of artifice. Maybe it was just that he was sorry for her. Maybe it was her money that was seducing him. Maybe he was just afraid for her. Or maybe it was just not having a woman for ten months. For ten months he had not touched a girl; he did not dare. He did not allow himself to smell a girl's hair or caress her skin, or kiss her mouth, because he was afraid it would be Frannie's burned skin he would feel, Frannie's burned mouth.

He could almost imagine being with a girl, if she were someone like Sally. Sally wasn't cerebral; Sally was a pretty body meant for dalliance, not for involving the mind. And she was making herself damned available, which was why he found himself thinking of her.

He had driven her out to the Castle several times since that first time. Her car was still laid up for repairs, and he couldn't very well refuse. Iris had to understand his position. She herself hadn't declared the place off limits to Sally, so how could he not give her a lift when she asked him?

On Monday after class, Sally spoke to him again about driving her. He couldn't resist saying it: "Why this burning interest in Nearing?"

"He's lonely, and I'm sorry for him," she said. "I guess if it hadn't been for me, Robbie would still be alive. I'm trying to make it up to him a little."

He didn't believe it. Maybe Nearing had some money stashed away. He had no one now to leave it to. It couldn't be Sally's desire to harass Iris. Iris never saw her when she came.

Another class was coming in, so he did not have to

reply, but she must have read something in his expression. Later that afternoon when they were in the car together, she said, "You don't like me very much. Why?"

He was disconcerted. "I hardly know you, Sally, except as a student. Why should I like or dislike you?"

"Because I'm not bad-looking, and you know I think you're attractive. But you act as if I didn't exist."

"I'm sorry." He managed a laugh. "I guess I've had my mind on other things. I've had a lot of work, a lot of new adjustments to make. And you're just a young chick, and I'm old."

"I don't buy that. You're not old. Thirty-two, three? You look older than you are. But I like that. Older men are into things, not like the kids at school."

"I'll file your declaration away for some time in the future. May I?" he said. "As soon as the pressure is off and I can find an hour for recreation."

"I know why you don't like me," she said. "Because she doesn't like me. And because she's an important person and rates with you, and who am I?"

"Come on, Sally. Lay off, will you? I won't give you any more lifts if you talk that way."

Her smile showed small even teeth between pink lips. She was pleased that she had roused him to a show of irritation. "You could at least ask me in to see your house. I used to go there when Robbie lived in it, but I hear you've changed it a lot."

"You're welcome to come any time."

"Tonight?"

114

"Not tonight. I have some work to do. Some other time, okay?"

He went past the gatehouse quickly, driving straight through to the garage where he'd let her off the other times.

She got out. "I'm going to take you up on that invitation. I want to see if you really mean it. Maybe I'll come and cook dinner for you. I'm a pretty good cook. Would you like that?"

Her smile mocking, she did not wait for his answer, but ran across the drive to the garage. He couldn't help but smile himself, even if she exasperated him. She was pretty, and she had made it very plain that she would like to be friendlier. Only he didn't want to get entangled with Sally, for many reasons. Not only because of Iris, but because of his own emotional state. As far as sex was concerned, he felt like an invalid who hadn't yet tested his strength; it had been burned out of him, with Frannie, and he didn't know what he was capable of. Now and then with Sally his desire would be briefly jolted, like the brief flare of a match, but he had no wish to pursue it.

Later in the week he drove her out to the Castle again, and she told him her car was ready and she wouldn't have to bother him anymore. "It was ready last week, but I didn't have the money to take it out," she said. "I didn't care. I'll miss driving with you." She gave him a sidelong glance. "Can I come to see your house tonight?"

"I'll be out. I'm giving Iris some tutoring."

No mocking retort. He was surprised, but she was silent, and only thanked him when he left her at the garage.

When Iris admitted him to the house that night, she looked different. He stared, and she said, "It's my hair. Do you like it?"

She wore it in bangs across her forehead. "Why did you do that? I liked the way you had it before."

She flushed. "I cut it off myself. I thought it looked prettier. I didn't think it looked so bad."

"It doesn't look *bad*," he said. "The other way seemed more like you, somehow."

But he had made her unhappy with his disapproval, he could tell. All during the hour her fingers kept straying to the fringe of hair, and he could see she was hardly listening. At last, when she didn't seem to be aware that he had even spoken to her, he said, as much out of irritation for his own tactlessness about her hair as for her inattention, "If you fussed with your hair less and listened more, Iris, you'd know I asked you a question."

She stood up abruptly. "I've got a headache. Maybe we'd better stop for tonight."

"By all means." He put his books together and left at once. Maybe it was just as well that she was reminded of their teacher-pupil relationship; the other was growing faster than they seemed able to control.

He was restless when he got home. I should have told her her hair was nice; I should have realized her skin is too thin for criticism. And yet, he didn't want her any different, that must be it; he liked the pale planes of her face uncluttered and clean. Curls and bangs were for girls like Sally.

Someone was tapping on the windowpane. He looked around and saw Sally's face peering in at him. There was nothing to do but open the door for her.

"You had to ask me in, didn't you? You didn't want to, but you knew it was rude not to."

He lifted his shoulders in resignation and stood aside to let her in. Her bright blue eyes darted everywhere. "You've done wonders, Doc! I can see why Nearing is upset about your living here!"

"I didn't know he was upset." It could still be Nearing who had vandalized the place; he hadn't entirely ruled him out, although since the balcony incident, it was the aunt who had become his prime suspect.

"I mean, I think he wanted it left the way it was. Robbie's dead, and the ruin this house was fitted what happened. Now everyone is talking about how you've fixed it up, and it's bringing everything back again."

"I didn't realize it would prove so interesting to everybody."

"Oh, they watch what goes on from the house—don't think they don't. Like Iris coming to see you. And your taking her to the movies."

"If they watch me, then you'd better be on your way, Sally. You don't want them talking about you."

"They've always talked about me. I don't mind anymore. I really came to ask you about Spenser." She sat down in his chair and opened her book. "By the time I figure out each word, I've stopped caring about what he's trying to say."

"There's a glossary in the back."

"I know, but . . ." She turned to Canto I, which they were reading in class. " 'Hypocrisie him to entrape,' " she read, " 'Doth to his home entreate.' " She made a face, "And listen to this: 'Who naught aghast, his mightie hand enhaunst: The stroke down from her head unto her shoulder glaunst.' Honestly, Doc. 'Glaunst'?"

She made a face, and he had to laugh. "It should do you good," he said. "Elevate your mind to higher things."

"Higher than what?"

He ignored her glinting look. "Why don't you read it out loud, the way I told you? It comes clear when you read it aloud."

"When *you* read it, it does. But not when *I* read it. Would you read a little?"

He hesitated. What the hell—the ham in him was flattered. He must enjoy the sound of his own voice. And the ham in him enjoyed her sitting there, pretending to listen raptly. Her eyes remained fixed on him, her face thoughtful, but he was sure she was not thinking of Spenser. The firelight softened the narrow fox shape of her face.

After a while he shut the book. "Okay," he said, "that's enough to keep you going for a while. Now clear out and let me relax."

"Can't you relax with me here? I like your fire and the music."

She was smiling at him. Abruptly, he reached down for her and pulled her to her feet. She allowed herself to slump against him, and before he knew it she kissed him.

"That's for giving me the lesson," she said.

Again, that flare of a match in him.

"Thanks. Now, on your way." He led her out to the hall and opened the door.

The light from his lamp fell full on Iris, standing there in a plaid storm jacket, her hair damp with the wet snow that had begun to fall.

For an instant, all three of them were struck silent. It was Sally who broke it, her words ringing out gaily.

"Hi, Miss Freebody. Doctor Sexton was just helping me with the Spenser. That's how democratic he is; he even has time for me. Bye, Doc," she said, her voice becoming fervent, "and thanks!"

"You're welcome," he said, trying not to sound put out. But he was. It was as if Sally had wanted this. Damn her, she probably did.

Iris made a move to go back, but he took her arm and held it firmly while Sally started her car, winked the headlights at them and then shot out through the gates before they had completely opened. The gates shut: they were in darkness and silence.

She said huskily, "I acted so stupidly. About the hair. I mean, it will grow out. I hoped you'd like it— I just wanted to tell you that."

"How you wear your hair isn't important. I shouldn't have said I didn't like it. Come in and let's talk a little."

She held back with unexpected stubbornness. "No. It's late." She shook free of his hand and walked hurriedly back toward the drive.

"Wait, Iris. I'll walk you back!"

But she didn't stop, didn't seem to hear him. Damn, he was freezing. He ran inside and picked up his mackinaw, pulling it on as he went after her. He didn't have time to get his boots at the back door, and his feet in moccasins were getting wet. "I'll probably get pneumonia," he panted, overtaking her.

She did not slow her walk, her head bent.

"Look," he said, grasping her arm again and making her stop, "she just barged in. If she had come to the office for help, I wouldn't have turned her away. I would have helped her. She's my student, damn it, Iris."

Her voice was muffled. "That isn't why she came, and you know it."

"Maybe it wasn't. But why should it matter to you?"

Still muffled, her answer came. "She wants to hurt me."

"Granted that she does, how does my helping her with Spenser hurt you?"

"You know why."

His feet were soaked and freezing, and his exasperation was mounting—with Sally for having precipitated this, with Iris for being so needlessly upset, with his own inability to cope. Should he tell her he wasn't interested in what Sally had to offer? Tell her he wasn't sure yet he wanted to get involved that way with anyone? Tell her he needed time, to forget, to heal . . .

"I have no right acting this way. I don't know why I am, or what made me come down to the gatehouse. It wasn't only to tell you I was ashamed about the way I behaved over my hair. I saw her car parked at the gatehouse. I had no right to barge in," she said a little wildly. "I probably wouldn't have come in. I probably would have turned around and gone home without a word except that you happened to open the door." She stopped and took a breath. "I suppose . . . I'm jealous."

"Jealous?"

"I don't know why I'm talking this way! It isn't like me at all! And I certainly don't expect you to understand how I feel. How could you, unless you felt the same way, and why should you?"

She stopped, and faced him. "Please don't think I expect you to. I mean, I know I'm not the kind of person people fall instantly and madly in love with." She looked miserable.

"Neither am I," he said gently, his head beginning to hurt.

She let him put his arm through hers, and they walked on without speaking. What to say? How not to hurt her?

She took a deep breath. "I must be out of my mind, behaving in such a childish and immature way. You've been very nice, and kind, but we hardly know each other."

121

"Right. And *you've* been very kind," he said. "And nice."

"I guess it was seeing her kiss you," she said. "I couldn't help it, you don't have any blinds, and you were standing there in the window where anyone could see you. I shouldn't have been there, but I was, and I saw. I thought of Robbie making love to her, and I thought that maybe one reason she let Robbie get her pregnant was to prove that he loved her more than me."

"I don't love Sally, " he said. "I don't even like her much."

"Don't feel you have to tell me!" she cried. "I mean, what reason do you have to tell me the details of your personal life—"

"Iris," he said, making her stop within the lights of the house, "you're engaged to be married, if not this year, then next year. I never wanted to burst in and mess up your plans. I don't want to be a presence in your life yet, if you know what I mean. Not for my sake, understand, but for your own. You can't properly evaluate your feelings about me. You've known Ralph longer than you've known me, and you're wondering if you're right about him now. Maybe you're wrong about both of us; maybe someone else will come along and make you see that one of these days."

Her eyes were level with his; she stared at him as if she were trying to read something behind his words.

He said, "Sometimes students feel about their teachers the way patients do about their psychiatrists.

It's a temporary thing, and once the classroom tie is broken, so is everything."

She said, "It isn't that way with me."

"How do you know I'm not a fortune hunter?"

She said slowly, "I don't think I would care if you were. I mean, I would care, but if it were the only way to make you . . . want to be with me, it would be better than nothing."

"You're not talking sense, Iris!"

"I know. But it's the way I feel."

He kissed her, almost without thinking. Snow settled on their hair, their eyelashes, blurring her face. Her cheeks were cold, and her wet hair caught on his collar. She was open, and yearning; unexpectedly, he felt tears sting his eyes.

They broke away. Her voice shook. "You don't owe me anything, Ian. I had no right to be jealous. Don't let what happened spoil your being here. Just forget it happened—everything is just the way it was before."

She fled toward the house, ungainly in her boots, sloshing through the wet snow.

He stared after her soberly, and then turned around and went home. I can't be in love with her. I don't want her as I wanted Frannie, or even any one of all those anonymous girls I would pass in the street, back when I still felt desire. As I wanted Sally for that moment when she leaned against me and I felt her sharp little breasts poking against me. . . .

He went into the gatehouse and locked the door and massaged his cold feet in front of the fire. I like her. I feel sorry for her. I'm scared that old biddy of an aunt will try something again if she thinks Iris is in love with me. I'm angry that she should be driven into a marriage that she doesn't really want, that she was pushed into, out of her own fears and insecurity and uncertainty.

But that didn't add up to desire. Desire was the elixir of life. Life was drab and leaden without it. How could you go through a lifetime with a woman you didn't desire? Slow death. He had desired Frannie; desire had run like an electric current through the ordinary, simple details of existence, transfiguring them. A trip to the supermarket, even—his arm grazing her breasts when he locked the car door, the back of her knees when she reached for something on a high shelf, her breath on his cheek when she whispered to him to get on *that* line, it was shorter . . . He'd be touched off like dry kindling, smoldering until he got her home.

Frannie had burned to death. He had wished her dead when he couldn't have her anymore. He had turned to a bitter, destructive fury, consumed by anger and helplessness as he had once been consumed by desire. Part of him had been destroyed with her. All of him, he had thought initially. But he was beginning to see that wasn't so; he was coming to life like a shoot that appears to be dead but when scraped with a fingernail is soft and green underneath after all. If he could love Iris, his life would be an easy pitch from now on. All that money. . . Not that he'd want to coast his whole life; that wasn't his bag. He believed in work as long as it was work that mattered to you. But imagine a life without pressure, without uncertainty, a case of What do you want to do? Just do it. As easy as that.

It was tempting; but was it enough?

# 8

*S*he must have been out of her mind to say the things she had, and that was why he was staying away. He had missed their next lesson. He had called her from school to say he was working late reading reports, but that he would try to see her on Tuesday—it all depended on how fast he could get the reports read and graded. She didn't see why he couldn't find an hour for her; it must be because she had alarmed him with the wild declarations she had made.

Somehow she had the feeling he would not come tonight either. She had worked herself up to a nervous state in her room before dinner, wondering whether or not he would come, and had only gone down to the dining room because otherwise Aunt Gladys would have been sure to appear at her door, asking what was wrong.

It was a silent meal. Aunt Gladys had grown sullen lately, as if it were she who had been put upon, not

Ralph, by the stalemate in their plans. She barely spoke, her plump face drawn into lines of injury, her eyes looking down into her plate. But at least once she brought up the subject of marriage, as if she had to bite down on a sore tooth.

She said, "Iris, if there's going to be a wedding I need time to plan for it. It wouldn't be fair to Ralph or you to have it be just some hurry-up little affair."

"Aunt Glad, we don't have to talk about it now, do we?"

"I don't mean it has to be final, or anything like that, but we could at least have some general plans ready so that if you changed your mind later on and decided to set a date after all, we would have some idea how to go ahead. Like, do we want a tent on the lawn, and who we would ask . . ."

Iris felt like sobbing—Ralph was so far from her thoughts—but she made herself answer. "Aunt Glad, whom would we need a tent for? We have hardly anyone to ask. No one in Mama's family would come; they're all angry at us. And Papa had just you."

"Ralph's father had family. I'm sure they would want to come. And people whom Ralph will be associated with. After all, he will want to show off his bride to them."

"It won't be this June," she said thickly. "I'm positive about that, so you really don't have to worry."

"Why hasn't *he* been here lately?" said Aunt Gladys. "He seems to have lost interest in giving you lessons."

Aunt Gladys must be listening in on the extension. Iris said, "He just missed one lesson. He's marking reports. I expect he'll be here tonight."

She escaped to her room as soon as she could and gave her hair another going-over with the brush. She found some toilet water that Ralph had given her last Christmas and sprayed it on. The telephone rang. Sexton. He couldn't come. He doesn't want to come. I've frightened him away.

A knock on her door. Evans. "Dr. Sexton is calling on the telephone, Miss Iris."

She swallowed several times before she could trust her voice to say hello.

"Iris? I'm terribly sorry, but I'm still at school. I'm groggy, and my eyes are about closing. Do you think you could read ahead and I'll try to go over everything next time we meet?"

She swallowed again. "Yes, of course," she said thickly.

He said briskly, "I'm sure you don't mind. Most of the students would be delighted if I didn't show up for class now and then. It will give you a night off."

"No, I don't mind," she said.

She heard the little click that meant someone had just hung up on the other extension, and then she hung up herself.

*Yes, Ian, I do mind. I mind very much. I mind terribly.* She saw him as he sat in the plush armchair opposite her; his odd thin face with the curling beard; the crepe-soled shoes turning up at the tips and mashed-looking on the bottom when he crossed one

128

leg across his thigh; the hazel eyes that could gleam with warmth and yet seem remote and fastidious at other times; his mouth when he smiled, more boyish than the rest of him—the mouth she had kissed.

She thought of his briefcase, ripped at the zipper, and wanted to cry. *For Christmas, could I buy you a new briefcase, or would that be in bad taste?* But you always gave your teacher a present at Christmas. Would he be embarrassed? Maybe she would never have another chance. Maybe the lessons would simply taper off, and one day he would suggest it was time to come back to class, and that would be the end of their meetings. He knew she would not ask him to go, even if the lessons stopped. Now that he had the gatehouse, he did not need to curry favor with her.

She couldn't bear the confines of her room. She pulled on her coat and ran downstairs and outside before Aunt Gladys could get off her sofa and come to the door of her sitting room to ask where she was going. She ran down the steps and onto the drive, her feet taking her inevitably toward the gatehouse, as if there were no other place they could go. Her heart quickened. She saw the back of a car sticking out through the trees. Perhaps he had come home. Perhaps she might just say hello, just glimpse his face to see if everything was all right between them, just make some light talk about what a shame he'd had so much work to do and that she was worried about him, something like that. . . .

The car was not Sexton's. It was Sally's battered old sedan. There was a light in Sexton's house. Her legs were numb, her heart was pounding heavily. She went around noiselessly to where the light came from. The kitchen. Sally was in Sexton's kitchen. The damp sodden leaves cushioned her feet so that Sally did not hear her as she looked in through the unshaded kitchen windows. Sally was at the stove, stirring something in a frypan. Her face was absorbed and she was sucking at her lip. Behind her, Sexton's wicker table was set for two.

Iris stepped back, and began to run. She must get away before Sexton returned. She would die of embarrassment if he found her here, spying on him. She ran up the drive as fast as she could and let herself into the house.

Aunt Gladys came into the hall as she pulled off her boots.

"What's the matter, Iris?"

"Nothing's the matter, Aunt Gladys," she said thinly. "Why do you always think something is the matter?"

Aunt Gladys was shaking her head. "Poor Iris. You found out. I was afraid you would sooner or later, and I swore I would never say a word about it because you would say I made it up. But now you've seen for yourself."

"I don't know what you're talking about," Iris said, going past her to the stairs.

"That man is no good. I knew it from the first moment I laid eyes on him. He used you for his own purposes, but now that he has what he wants he can play around with that little slut, and he has a nice

130

private place where they can meet. She won't be the last, you can be sure. There'll be a whole string of girls coming here. Why do you think he wanted to be far away from town, where no one could see him and spread any gossip about him? You're only a babe in arms, Iris, but I'm glad you found out before you could be really hurt—"

"I don't want to hear any more!" Iris cried, running up the stairs.

"At least there's been no harm done, and Ralph doesn't have to know what's been going on while he's away. You can be sure I won't say anything. You can pick up again where you left off, and he'll be none the wiser."

At the top of the stairs she bumped into Coffey, whose eyes glittered with anger. "What is she saying to you, love? You mustn't pay any attention to her. That woman is evil. She'd destroy you to get her hands on that money—"

"Ssh, Coffey," she said. "Please, I don't want to hear about her or anyone else. Won't you please let me alone?" She shook her arm free of Coffey's hand and rushed into her room and slammed the door, leaning against it as if she could repel any intruders with her weight.

She could hear Aunt Gladys stomping up the stairs, hear her pant furiously, "Will you mind your own business, you senile old woman! Go to your room at once and leave my niece alone!"

"You're no friend to her! You never were! Coming here to squeeze what you can out of her—"

"I'll have you thrown out! You're only a servant in this house and don't you forget it. You'll be put in a home where they'll know how to treat senile old women. Tie you up in a straitjacket, they will—"

"Iris! Iris!"

She opened her door. "Come, Coffey, I'll take you upstairs," she said, and took her arm.

"You won't let her put me in a home, Iris?"

"Of course not," she whispered. "This is your home for as long as you live."

"Be careful, Iris. She'll do you harm if she can."

"Don't worry about me, Coffey."

She settled Coffey in her chair, tucked the shawl over her legs and turned on the television for her.

"Turn it off. Don't want that nonsense. I've got to keep my eyes and ears open all the time, Iris. I don't want her to hurt you."

"She won't. You mustn't worry."

She found Coffey's jar of sweets and the newspaper, and fixed the light so she could read, and let herself out.

Aunt Gladys was sitting in Iris's room, weeping. Iris sighed, and sat down opposite her.

"Iris, why do you let that crazy old woman say the things she does? Don't you have any regard at all for me?"

"I do, Aunt Glad. She's been sick, and she's frightened. You mustn't mind what she says."

"I have feelings, too. You're the only flesh and blood I have left. Ralph is my stepson and I raised him and did everything I could for him, but I know he never really loved me the way he should. You're different, Iris. You're the daughter I never had, and I want to love you like a daughter, and I was hoping you would love me a little, too."

"I do, Aunt Glad."

Aunt Gladys found her handkerchief. "You think I meant to spoil it for you when I warned you against that man. I just didn't want you to be hurt. I've been around a lot longer than you have and I've run against his type before, and I knew you were no match for him. You're too sensitive to handle men like that. I only want you to be happy. I know Ralph can make you happy, and I'm afraid you'll spoil it with your crush on this conniver—"

"Don't call him that. You don't know what he's like."

"What would you call a man who wheedles his way in here to live rent-free in that lovely little house—"

"It was a wreck when he moved in."

"—and then proceeds to have girls in there, as if you didn't exist?"

"Aunt Gladys, he's free to do whatever he wants in his own house. I didn't make any conditions when I said he could stay there."

"But what about you? Shouldn't he have any regard for your feelings?"

Iris's throat was filling up. Aunt Gladys's sympathy was almost harder to bear than her bludgeoning. She mustn't break down. "He doesn't owe me anything," she said. "He's told me not to rush into anything, that I don't know him and he doesn't know me. That's why he may be staying away, because he suspects I'm in love with him."

"You're in love with him?" Aunt Gladys's face had turned white.

Iris stood up. Why had she told her? It was as if she needed to say the words out loud to someone, and there was no one else but Aunt Gladys. "I think I'll go to bed now," she said. "I have a little headache."

"Oh, my God," said Aunt Gladys. "You poor thing. What's going to happen now?"

"Aunt Gladys, do you mind . . ."

"I'm going now. Oh, Iris, you poor thing. It's the worst thing that could have happened to you."

"I'm going to try to get some sleep. I'm fine otherwise, Aunt Gladys. I just have this bit of a headache."

"Isn't there anything I can do for you? I'd like to do something for you, Iris."

"Nothing, Aunt Glad. Thanks."

Aunt Gladys left. Iris tried to read after she was gone, but the words didn't reach her. She got up and went out on her newly repaired balcony, and leaned out to see through the leafless trees to the gatehouse. His car was there now, too. He was having his supper with her at the yellow table, offering her wine, the hi-fi filling the house richly, the smell of his fire perfuming it. He'll want her to go to bed with him, the way Robbie did. And why not? She's pretty, and she knows how to act with a man; she's not a clumsy, tongue-tied oaf of a girl like me. She drew back. Bitterness filled her. She wept, in a different way from the way she had wept for Robbie.

She undressed and got into bed, but she couldn't sleep. She put her light on again and tried to read, but the print blurred. She went to her balcony and leaned out again. Sexton's house was dark. She could no longer see if there were one or two cars there.

There was a tap on her door. "Iris?"

Wearily she went to the door and opened it. It was Aunt Gladys, carrying a cup of hot cocoa. "I saw your light and I saw you out on your balcony, and I knew you couldn't fall asleep. Try this, angel. I put one of my sleeping pills in it. Drink it down and you'll go right to sleep."

"I don't feel like having any cocoa, Aunt Gladys."

"You'll see how much better you'll feel. I always used to fix this for Ralph when he'd get wound up before an examination. That boy always wanted to come out on top, and it made him very tense. He'd go right to sleep after this, and wake up with his head clear as a bell and ready for anything. Do what I tell you, Iris lamb."

She drank it down. It was so bitter that she did not finish it. Aunt Gladys took the cup from her, and waited until she had climbed back into bed. She covered her with the blanket, and kissed her.

"You'll see how much different everything will seem in the morning, angel."

Her heart was still pounding heavily when Aunt

Gladys turned out her light and left, and she wondered if the pill would work. Her mouth felt dry, and she started to get up to get some water, when her legs gave way beneath her. She reached for the night table for support, but her hand struck something cold, glass, and it fell and shattered against the parquet floor. She tried to get back into bed, but slipped down. Blackness settled over her.

Later, she stirred, and felt icy cold. I'm sick, she thought, but she couldn't move or call out. She vomited, and then sank into darkness again.

# 9

*H*e saw the light in the gatehouse as he drove up, and his first thought was: Someone's broken in again. His heart thudded as he tried to convince himself that he might have left the light burning; it was dark these mornings when he went away and he might have forgotten to turn the kitchen light off. He turned the key with a tense hand, and almost at once smelled cooking. Before he could collect his thoughts, Sally came out into the hall.

She made a face when she saw his expression. "You don't have to look so mad. I only wanted to surprise you."

"Sally, I've had a long day, and forty reports still to be read." How the hell had she come in? He kept the doors and windows locked tight when he left.

"Well, I have your dinner cooked, so all you have to do is sit down and eat. I even mixed you a martini. Sometimes I make them at the café when the barman is busy, and no one can tell the difference."

He supposed he was being surly. Had it been anyone else but Sally he might have laughed the whole incident off, accepted what he couldn't do anything about. But he was wary of her now, and he had hoped that with her car fixed he wouldn't be running into her again out of class. He put his books away, came back into the kitchen and took his place in silence. He drank his martini too fast while she spooned spaghetti and meatballs onto his plate.

The gin reached him speedily; the glass was too large, and the drink too generous. He relaxed enough to feel ashamed of his surliness. "You cook well, Sally."

"But you wish I hadn't come."

"I don't like anybody barging in, I admit it. Even if it were an old friend, I'd expect him to ask me beforehand if he planned to come into my house when I wasn't there."

She managed to look contrite. "I wanted it to be a surprise. A way to say thank-you for all the times you drove me out here."

"I appreciate the thought. And thanks. But I'm dog-tired, Sally, and when you're that tired it's an effort to be sociable. The meal was really great," he said, pushing himself from the table.

She wanted to clean up herself, but he thought it would send her on her way faster if he helped, so he took a towel. The oversized martini was making itself felt, or else it was the combination of gin and fatigue. Whatever the cause, a lassitude spread up from his feet, filling him almost pleasantly. He grew aware of her hips swelling under the tight jeans. Their bodies seemed to touch often, accidentally, or on purpose, whose purpose he wasn't sure.

She didn't go when they'd finished in the kitchen, but went ahead of him to the living room. "I even got the fire ready for you, see? I used to be a girl scout when I was a kid, and I bet you can't lay a better one. A better fire, I mean." She laughed up into his face, kneeling in front of the hearth and touching a match to the pile of wood. It blazed up beautifully. "See?" She was still kneeling.

"It's a beauty. Now you better go home, Sally."

"Why are you so afraid for me to be here?" She leaned back, resting on her elbows.

She was pushing those hard pointed breasts up at him again. He said, "Sally, your routine went out with the silent movies. You ought to know better. Come on, you're irresistible, but some other time."

"What other time, Doc?" she whispered. "Will there ever be a better time?"

He leaned over to grasp her, but she resisted with unexpected strength, or maybe it was because he was unsteady. He fell to his knees over her, and she clasped her arms around his neck and drew him down. Touching her was a painful low blow to his body. He gave up struggling within himself. He was tired, and she was asking for it, and his brain was foggy, and what the hell did it matter?

Someone was pounding hard on the window. He turned his head, and saw a gargoyle face flattened against the glass. His heart almost stopped beating.

"Nearing," whispered Sally.

He got up, arranging his clothes desperately as he went to the door. He turned to make sure Sally was on her feet. He felt like a kid, embarrassed, humiliated. How much had Nearing seen? The chairs blocked part of the fireplace, but he could have seen enough. Sexton opened the door.

"I want to speak to her," Nearing said, brushing past him. He stood in the living-room door. "Give me back my key you stole."

She tried to laugh. "I didn't steal it. Just borrowed it. I knew you didn't need it."

"Stole it from my key board," Nearing said furiously, "when my back was turned."

"Here, take it," she said, fishing it out of the pocket of her jeans. "I only wanted to make Dr. Sexton dinner. For being so nice to me."

So that was how she had gotten in—with Nearing's key.

Nearing was looking at him with contempt. "Thought you professors had more sense than to mix with this kind."

"Now you look here—" she began.

"She's a whore," Nearing said harshly. "She killed my boy."

"You were more to blame than me! If he hadn't been so scared of you, he wouldn't have done it!"

"Whore!" Nearing moved on her, his arm raised.

Sexton managed to get between them. "Not in my house, Nearing. Look, you got what you came for. Now leave."

140

For an instant Nearing stared at him, stocky and foursquare, like a bull, his eyes red and angry. His arm dropped. He said to her, "Now I know why you've been hanging around. I thought you'd changed and wanted to make it up with me. You sure fooled me. You're still a tramp. What you wanted was *him*."

He turned and went out heavily.

He and Sally were left, facing each other. He felt sick to his stomach, and it was an effort to make himself speak.

"I'm sorry for what happened tonight, Sally. We mustn't let it happen again."

She came close to him and put her arms around his waist. "Why are you sorry? I'm not. I never said there were any strings, did I? Unless you're afraid of Nearing. Is that it?"

He disengaged her and held her off with both hands on her arms. "Sally, we can't give each other anything. I don't want this kind of bloodless encounter. I'm not in love with you, and you're not with me." Her eyes made fun of him, and he supposed he sounded like a stuffed shirt. "It was my fault as much as yours, maybe more. The only way we can be sure it won't happen again is for you not to come here anymore. I mean that, Sally. I don't want you here again."

The soft, teasing look left her face. "You *are* afraid. Not of Nearing. Of her. That's it, isn't it?"

"If I'm afraid of anyone, it's of you, Sally," he said soberly. "I can't handle you. I don't like what I can't handle."

"You don't fool me," she said. "You think you have

a chance with her, a chance at all that money. You professors don't do so well, I hear, and I bet she doesn't look half as bad when you think of those millions. Right, Doc?"

She was pulling on her coat, looking for her boots in a corner of the hall as she talked.

"She isn't going to like it when she finds out about tonight. You're not going to look so wonderful to her now, Doc."

She slammed out the door, and in a moment he heard the gates open and the metallic whine of her motor getting started.

Fatigue had left him, or maybe he was just numb to it now. He didn't even try to go to sleep; he knew it was impossible. He couldn't listen to music, and his eyes were too tired to read. Get good and drunk, he told himself. He got out a bottle of Scotch and a glass, poured himself a drink and waited for it to have its effect. It had none at all. He poured himself another.

She would tell Iris about tonight, he was sure, in some way. Anonymous letter, that would be her style. Or maybe a telephone call, out in the open, her teasing, little-girl voice lingering on the details, embellishing as she went along out of the richness and variety of her experience—and from tonight he could guess at the variety—while Iris listened, unable to put the phone down, the way the hypnotized follow the hands of the hypnotist.

He had another drink. He was still cold sober, but sweating now, and he put the bottle away, got his jacket, wrapped a muffler around his neck and went out to gulp some fresh air.

The Freebody house was a blaze of lights.

He stared, stupefied, and then looked down at his watch. Two o'clock. It couldn't be a party. There were no cars. Even as he stood there, headlights raked the drive where he stood, the gates slid open, and a car came through. He watched it speed up the driveway toward the house. Ralph? Were they waiting for him? He just managed to get a glimpse of the license plate. It had "MD" beside the number, with the small white shield of Aesculapius mounted above. Involuntarily, he began to run, following the car to the house.

The front door was ajar. He rang, and Evans, in a bathrobe over his pajamas, let him in. Evans's face looked frightened.

"What happened?"

"It's Miss Iris—"

He didn't wait, but ran up the stairs to her room. The bedroom door was closed, but in the sitting room he saw the aunt weeping in a chair, and the maid Agnes bending over her with a yellow bottle of what looked like smelling salts. The aunt looked up when she saw him, her face mottled red and puffy with weeping.

"It's your fault!" she cried. "It's because of you that she did it! I knew you would bring trouble as soon as I saw you!"

"What the hell happened here?" he said. "Is the doctor in there?"

He went past her and opened the bedroom door. Iris

was in her bed, but his view of her was blocked by the man bending over her. The man lifted his head. "Wait outside, please," he said curtly.

"Are you the doctor?"

"Yes. Nichols. Please stay outside."

"Is she all right? What happened?"

"I'll talk to you later. It's too soon to tell."

Sexton went out, his legs thick and numb, like wooden limbs.

From the shadows Miss Coffey emerged. She was shaking, and as she drew him with her out into the hall it was less to steer him out of the fray than to lean on him for support. "Iris may die," she said in a broken whisper. "She drank a whole bottle of sleeping pills."

"Why?" he cried. "Why?"

Her fingers dug into him. "*She* says it's because of you. *She* says its because you're carrying on with Sally Lucas, and Iris couldn't bear it."

"I'm not carrying on with anybody," he said, even if it was a lie, technically. What did a gin-clouded few minutes signify? "I told Iris that I don't care a damn for Sally Lucas."

"Maybe she didn't believe you," Coffey said. "Maybe you didn't say it strong enough. You didn't come tonight, and she felt very bad. She went down to your house looking for you. I saw her. And I saw her come running back as if someone were after her. She was half out of her mind, I could tell when I saw her, even though she tried to hide it."

He felt the blood come up into his face. When had

she gone down to the house? What had she seen through the unshaded windows?

Dr. Nichols came out, and went at once to Mrs. Forsher. "I'm going to give you something to sleep, Mrs. Forsher. There's nothing you can do for her. I'll be with her at the hospital."

"I can go to the hospital with her! I should be with her! She should have someone of her own flesh and blood with her if she dies—"

"She isn't going to die," Dr. Nichols said.

The aunt's eyes rolled up in their sockets. The doctor snatched the smelling salts from Agnes and put them to Mrs. Forsher's nose until she choked and gasped. "You better take care of yourself," he said sternly. "You're overweight, and at your age you should start thinking of your heart." He was rolling up her sleeve as he spoke; he filled a needle and jabbed it into her arm. "Take her back to her room, Agnes, and help her get to bed. This stuff should work fast."

Sexton cornered the doctor. "How did Iris get her hands on sleeping pills? She had a nervous breakdown a few years ago. Was it wise to leave a large supply of drugs where she could get at them?"

The doctor looked at him sharply. "You the man living in the gatehouse?"

He nodded.

The doctor said, "The sleeping pills were Mrs. Forsher's."

The aunt heard her name, and turned in the doorway. She said huskily, "I only gave her one, in a cup of cocoa. She was so upset tonight, poor thing, so worried and unhappy, and when she couldn't sleep I made her a cup of cocoa and put a sleeping pill in it."

"One?" He looked at the doctor.

"Obviously, she had many more. I found the empty bottle on the floor near her bed," Dr. Nichols said.

"I don't understand. Where did she get the others?" Sexton asked.

"I had them in the pocket of my robe when I fixed the cocoa," the aunt said. "She must have taken them out when I wasn't looking. I was upset myself tonight for her. If you had half a conscience," the aunt cried, "you wouldn't have treated her the way you did. She wanted to die tonight. I swear, she wanted to die!"

Coffey spoke. "If you knew she wanted to die, why didn't you stay with her? Why did you leave her alone? *I* didn't go to sleep tonight. I walked up and down outside her room, listening. I was afraid for her. That's how I heard her fall."

"And a good thing," said the doctor. "We'll be able to pump out whatever pills are left in her in the hospital. She was lucky that she chucked up so much of it right away. If she hadn't brought a good deal of it up, her pulse and heart wouldn't be this strong."

They could hear a car racing up the drive.

"That'll be the ambulance," Nichols said, and went to the window to look down. He left the room at once, and they could hear him calling from the head of the stairs, "Up here!"

The two orderlies brought a stretcher. In the bed-room they wrapped Iris's inert figure in a blanket and

146

lifted her onto the stretcher and carried her out. Sexton caught only a glimpse of her parted mouth and white cheek in a small fold of blanket that remained open.

"I'll follow in my car," he said to Nichols. "Will I have any problem getting into the hospital?"

Dr. Nichols hesitated, looking at him sharply. Then he said, "I'll tell them you're coming," and left after the orderlies.

Mrs. Forsher was still weeping into her handkerchief as Agnes led her from the room. Miss Coffey watched in silence until she was gone.

"She's lying," she said then. "Crocodile tears, that's what they were. She wants Iris dead, and she had something to do with what happened tonight. Don't know exactly, but her hand was in it somehow."

He was anxious to get to the hospital. He was exhausted, and still shaken from the shock of what happened. He said wearily, "Is there anything you know, Miss Coffey, for a *fact*?"

"She gave Iris those sleeping pills, didn't she?"

"She gave her one."

"So *she* says. You believe that? Where's the cocoa cup? She took it back to the kitchen and washed it out with soap powder. Fat lazy thing, she never lifted a finger to wash anything. Ask Agnes. Or the cook. Ask them when she last set foot in the kitchen. Cigarettes and ashes all over the sofa in the sitting room where she lies about all day, doesn't even reach for the ashtray, tub of lard that she is. Why would she go down to the kitchen to make cocoa, and then bring back the

147

cup and scour it when she could have the maids do it? Because she wanted to put those pills in it, and then wash the evidence away. Iris was too beside herself to know what she was drinking. If Mrs. Forsher said she was giving her one pill, Iris wouldn't know enough to ask why it was so bitter. Planted the empty bottle on the night table herself, where Iris knocked it over. She watches them serials on TV all the time, gets ideas from them."

He listened. He said finally, "Look, Miss Coffey, don't say a word about this to anyone."

Her glance was shrewd and angry. "You going to protect her, that murderer?"

"I want to protect *you*. And Iris," he said quietly. "If you hadn't been watching Iris so closely tonight, she might have died. She needs you alive. If what you say is correct, then Mrs. Forsher might try something on you next."

"I keep my eyes and ears open all the time. She can't do anything without my knowing it. I don't hardly sleep anymore nights. Just catnaps. And I walk around the rest of the night."

Nevertheless the balcony had collapsed, and now Iris was nearly poisoned. He took a breath. "You're wonderful, Miss Coffey. Just keep up the good work. And don't let anything happen to you."

She clutched his arm. "But sometimes I'm . . . sick. I mean to watch her every minute, but—"

"I know," he said, leading her to the stairs. "Maybe you should keep your door locked when Iris isn't here. I want to see her now, Miss Coffey."

He left her watching him as he ran down the stairs. He got his car and drove to the hospital.

They were working on Iris in the emergency room, and he sat outside in the hall listening to the occasional cries that disturbed the sleeping quiet, the occasional jarring call over the loudspeaker for some doctor, the sound outside of the ambulance taking off again.

They must have taken her from the emergency room to a bedroom through another corridor, because it was some time later when Dr. Nichols came for him. The doctor took him upstairs, opened a door and showed him Iris lying in bed, her skin no longer gray but still pale.

She was awake. She turned her head and saw him. "Sexton," she said thickly.

"Ian."

"Funny my getting sick like this, so suddenly," she whispered. "How did you know, Ian?" She spoke as if her throat were sore.

Nichols motioned him not to answer. "Dr. Sexton can talk to you tomorrow, Iris."

But Ian reached for her hand to press it, and on impulse put it to his lips. He felt her hand start in his at his touch.

On their way out Dr. Nichols said, "She has no recollection at all of taking those pills."

"That's unusual, isn't it?"

"Sometimes they don't realize how many they've taken," Dr. Nichols explained. "They'll start with one, and then wake up groggily and take some more, and

149

lose count. But that was a hell of a lot of pills to swallow, unless they were dissolved in something."

In a cup of cocoa? He didn't want to express his suspicions to Dr. Nichols until he had first discussed them with Iris. She felt unnecessarily guilty for too many things already, and she would have to be convinced first that her aunt had a hand in it.

"Odd, though, that Iris would have the impression that she was *sick*—I mean, had developed some sort of illness," Dr. Nichols said.

The doctor, it seemed, might have suspicions of his own. Indeed, how *could* Iris have thought she was sick if she had tried to kill herself? Sexton wondered about that himself.

# 10

*H*e never got to his first two morning classes. He wouldn't have been much good if he'd made them anyway, after two hours of sleep. It had been five when he crawled into bed. He managed to get to the telephone when his alarm rang at seven and told the secretary that he wouldn't be in till the freshman survey course at two. He swallowed two aspirins and went back to sleep.

When he awoke again his head was clear. He showered and shaved mechanically while his mind was busy trying to put the events of last night into perspective. He drank his coffee standing at the window, and frowned at the exquisite highlight of snow that had been traced on each bare twig and branch. He *had* been busy last week with mid-semester reports. On the other hand, he *had* deliberately stayed away from Iris, to try and slow down the breakneck pace at which they seemed to be moving toward each other. Would that, and seeing Sally in his house, push her to the point where she would want to die?

He didn't believe it. He could believe she was delicately balanced after her nervous breakdown, but that was five years ago, and she was young and healthy. While she might be overly sensitive and even inclined to overreact, he was sure she had sufficiently recovered not to try anything drastic.

It had to be the aunt, then. Mrs. Forsher might be stupid, and not adroit, but that did not make her any the less dangerous. One of her clumsy attempts might succeed. She was a driven woman, almost frantic; you could see that just by looking at her. And she was getting more desperate. The balcony episode could be dismissed as carelessness; that she had deliberately ignored the mason's warning might never have been revealed if he hadn't examined the balcony with them. But she had admitted making the cocoa and putting a sleeping pill in it, probably banking on the probability that Iris would die. Now she had to depend on Iris's own uncertainty about how the rest of the pills were swallowed. Suppose she knew that Iris suspected her; suppose she knew her fate was now held in Iris's hands. Wouldn't she be desperate enough to try something soon again?

He would have to talk to Iris. He would have to make her aware of her danger.

He went to his two o'clock class. His thoughts about Iris had driven Sally from his mind until now. Now he wondered: Would she come to class? Or would she be too uncomfortable to face him after last night?

Not Sally. He had known the answer all along. Sure enough, she marched in smiling, and turned her head to look full at him as she went to her seat. There was satisfaction in her smile. It read: Mission accomplished. And that mission had not been to get him to make love to her; he was convinced of that when he saw her smile. He had given her a weapon to clobber Iris with. That was all she had ever wanted from him, and if he hadn't been too distracted with other problems he might have realized it sooner.

He started the lesson. At least his conscience wasn't going to bother him. She had managed to erase most of his feelings of guilt. The problem now was to get her to be quiet. Plead with her on the basis of decency? Threaten, as a member of the faculty? He would have to reach her, somehow.

But he didn't get the chance to try his luck with her that day, because when the bell rang he saw Dean Bemis waiting outside his door.

"Can you come into my office for a moment, Sexton?"

He followed Bemis out and across the road to his office and sat down in the chair Bemis pointed to. Bemis looked uncomfortable, fumbling in a drawer of his desk.

"Everything all right, Sexton? Adjusting to life in Freebody?"

"Fine." That was patently not what was on Bemis's mind.

153

"How do you like living on the Freebody estate? I hear you've become good friends with Miss Freebody."

"Working out well," he said. How did Bemis know about his being good friends with Iris?

"Look, this is somewhat unpleasant," Bemis said. "Still, you have to know about it." He had removed a letter from the drawer and was tapping his hand with it. Now he held it out to him. "This came in the afternoon mail. It was mailed in Freebody this morning."

Expensive vellum, cream, a painstaking Spencerian penmanship, *i*'s dotted, *t*'s crossed, loops rounded. It said:

Dear Dean Bemis:
I think you should be informed about the morals of the members of your faculty. You must realize that the parents of young girls want to be sure that their children are in good hands when they attend classes, and not subject to the after-school attentions of corrupt men, possibly rapists. Ask Dr. Sexton about the students who visit him at the gatehouse.

It was signed, "A Friend of Freebody College."

For a moment Sexton was too stunned to speak, and then he gave a short, explosive laugh.

"Convey anything to you?" said Bemis. "I mean, it could be a lot of smoke for a little fire."

"You put your finger on it precisely."

"Then there is something specific?"

He looked up at Bemis. "Does my after-school life, as the letter put it, matter to the college?"

154

Bemis seemed put out. "Of course not. Those years are behind us, I hope. Still, if it became a matter of scandal—and you know, Sexton, there's a danger in tangling with a student, especially a young girl. I'm saying this now for your own sake."

"There's nothing for the college to get uptight about. I give you my word. I'm not interested in any of my students."

Bemis looked relieved. "Good. Then we'll just forget about it."

Sexton hesitated as he was on his way out. The letter could be from Sally. In fact, it most likely was, and if it was, there was a chance of some flak to follow. Bemis might just as well be prepared. "There's one girl in one of my classes who's been—well—say, overcordial. I think it's finished, though. At least I made it plain I'm offering no encouragement. She might even be the one who wrote the letter."

"Who is she?"

Sexton shook his head. "What would be the point of my telling you?"

Bemis looked less happy. "We wouldn't like a scandal, Sexton. After all, you've become close to the Freebodys."

Sally might not have written the letter. The more he thought of it the more likely it seemed that Sally's strategy would be a telephone call—or she might contrive a meeting when she was visiting Nearing. It was the aunt, probably. The handwriting was a woman's, which ruled out Nearing. The aunt would buy this kind of expensive paper.

He left school early; he had phoned the hospital to ask after Iris and was told she would be leaving for home by noon, and he wanted to see her as soon as possible. He did not even stop at the gatehouse, but drove directly to the Castle.

Evans let him in, but had him wait until he found out if Iris was able to see visitors.

He paced the hall.

The door of the sitting room opened, and Mrs. Forsher came out. Her hair was not at its usual gilded height, but hung wispily about her neck, and her prominent eyes were embedded in puffy discolored skin. "You might have the decency not to force your presence on Iris anymore," she said thinly. "But I suppose decency is too much to expect from a man like you."

It was the way she spoke that evoked the manner of the letter. He was almost sure. He threw the question at her to see her reaction. "What can you expect from a corrupt rapist?"

Color flooded her skin at hearing the words of the letter. She gaped at him for an unbearable moment, and then she went back into the sitting room and shut the door hard.

"Miss Freebody says you can go up."

He went upstairs soberly. So it *was* the aunt. It must have been the aunt who'd vandalized the house, too. Come to think of it, that type of sly, secretive attack wasn't Nearing's way. Nearing would have bludgeoned his way in and slashed his mattress in front of him in a blind rage. The vandalism had been sneaky, like the letter. And she couldn't stop now. She was in a corner, and dangerous, and everything she wanted was inexorably slipping away from her.

"Hello, Ian."

Iris was in a long robe, lying among pillows on the sofa in her sitting room. She looked tired, but her smile was the same. When he bent to kiss her, she took his hand and made him sit beside her.

"You're better, I can see. No ill effects at all?"

"Just my throat. From the tubes they put down. They said I had to rest this afternoon, but when Wolfe, our chauffeur, came with Aunt Gladys, I walked out to the car and felt fine."

How to bring up the matter of Aunt Gladys? He got up and began to pace again.

"Are you in a hurry? Do you have work to do? I'm taking up so much of your time," she said ruefully.

He shook his head, sat down again on a chair where he could face her and see her expression. "Iris, how did it happen? Do you know?"

"Dr. Nichols told me I took too many sleeping pills." Her face had become withdrawn, her voice flat.

"Did you?"

She made a gesture. "I may have. I don't remember."

"You didn't even *have* any sleeping pills, did you?"

Again that gesture of helplessness. "Aunt Glad says I took the bottle from the pocket of her robe. She says she noticed it was missing that night, but thought she might have left it in the kitchen when she was fixing the cocoa."

"Do you believe that?" he said.

"I don't know," she said. "Ian, I'm all right now. Let's not talk about it anymore."

He digested the import of her words incredulously. "Then, you're not going to do anything about it? You're going to let this situation continue, put your life in danger every day? Let her try again?"

In the silence he could hear the heavy wheezing breath outside the door. Iris heard it, too, and lifted her head. In an instant he went to the door and wrenched it open, but Mrs. Forsher's back was toward him, retreating down the hall to her room.

He shut the door and said exasperatedly, "You know she listens at your door! She listens in on the extension when I call you—someone does, and who else could it be? I hear the click when she puts the phone down! You may not believe that she deliberately waited for the balcony to collapse, but how can you doubt that she tried to kill you last night?"

"I don't know what to do," she said in a low voice.

He stopped and made himself take a deep breath. "Why don't you speak to your uncle, the lawyer, and ask him what you should do. Tell him about the balcony, and tell him it was just carelessness on her part, if you want to. And tell him about the sleeping pills, and what she says happened. But remember—tell him that you don't recall taking them. You can even mention the vandalism to the gatehouse. Ask him what he thinks."

She turned her face away. He took another deep breath. "Your uncle may speak first as a lawyer and say, sure, you have no case against her. Where's the proof? You'd have to get a detective in to find any proof, if

158

you *could* find it. But then he would speak to you as your onetime guardian and still friend, and tell you to get her out of your house!"

"I can't," she said.

"You can't?" he exclaimed in disbelief. "Damn it, I'd like to speak to your uncle myself!"

"No! Don't do that!" she cried.

Her words quieted him. He was taking a lot for granted, wasn't he? Who the hell was he to interfere in her life? Now it was he who was accelerating their relationship, assuming he had the right to move in and take over.

He stood up. "I'm sorry I'm butting into your affairs," he said. "I don't know why I imagined I should." He moved toward the door. "Iris, rest up. Let me know when you're ready for another lesson."

"Ian, don't go."

He hesitated at the door.

"Please come back. I don't know how to explain it."

He came back and sat down.

"I don't want to be cruel to her. I've done enough harm to her. And to Ralph."

"*You've* harmed *her?*" he said. "How? You've given her a home, treated her generously, even lavishly, given her a chance to put money aside for herself—and I gather she has done just that. You, or at least the family, have paid for her stepson's education—at Harvard, no less—setting him up for life. You call that harm?"

"I owe it to her. And to Ralph. They were good to me."

"Sure they were. But how *much* do you owe them?

159

Does she have to succeed in murdering you before you've paid what you owe?"

"You said yourself there's no proof," she said faintly.

"No, and there's no proof that she sent an anonymous letter to Dean Bemis, suggesting that I was corrupting the morals of my girl students!"

She leaned forward. She whispered, "Ian, she couldn't have!"

"She could have," he said grimly. "I have no proof. But I'd swear it was she. She knows I'm on to her, and she wants to get me out. This isn't the time to upset you—" he could see she was shaken by the letter "—and I wouldn't have told you except that I don't know how to convince you that she's panicked enough to stop at nothing."

She reached for his hand. "Ian, try to understand."

"I'll try."

"And don't tell me I'm neurotic."

"I don't think you are."

"Ian, all my life I've brought nothing but . . . grief to people."

She saw his expression, and squeezed his hand hard so he would not interrupt. "Let me say it all. When I was a baby, someone tried to kidnap me. They caught him and sent him to prison for life. He may still be in prison. He was in his twenties, and very poor. He asked for a million dollars. Ian, Robbie killed himself. No matter what you say, I know I was as much to blame as anyone. If he had told me about Sally I would have told my father and maybe I could have got the money for him. But he didn't tell me about Sally, because he didn't want me to know. He was ashamed, for *me*. Maybe he did believe we might be married one day. I believed it, then."

Her eyes searched his face.

"I was even a disappointment to my mother. Maybe if I'd been the beautiful child she wanted, she would have stayed home more with me. But I never interested her."

"Now you *are* being neurotic."

"But it's how I feel. Can I help it if it's the way I *feel*? My father asked Aunt Glad to come here, because I needed her. And after making her share her life with me, shall I tell the police that she wants to kill me? Ever since she came she's dreamed of Ralph and me getting married. Can you imagine what it did to her when I put it off? And then when I told her that . . . that I was . . . very fond of you—"

"You told her that? When?"

"That day. Yesterday. I went down to your house and saw Sally fixing dinner for you."

He had difficulty hiding his relief. That was all she had seen, then, Sally fixing dinner. "I wonder if that was what drove her off the deep end," he said.

She was silent, but she didn't deny it either.

"Iris, you must see that she could have done it. And if you do, you have to take steps to protect yourself."

"I *can't*, Ian. Don't you see? All these years, when she was like, well, the mistress here . . . even Ralph, it's as if he already owned it all, he loves it so. They both do. They feel so grand and important. How can I do it to them?"

"You can and you have to, because it's your life that's in jeopardy!" In desperate urgency he cried out, "I can't let you take this chance! You've got to do something!"

Color mounted in her cheeks at his passion. She looked at him as if she wanted to believe it. "Does it matter so much to you, Ian?"

He grew quiet. He said slowly, "Yes. It does."

She swallowed, and her eyes glistened. "I'll talk to her. I will tell her. I'll ask her to leave."

He let his breath out. "When?"

"I don't know. I'll find the moment when I can break it to her. Something will come up, some opportunity—"

"Iris, there isn't time. You have to act at once. Every moment means you're in danger, and there's no one here who can protect you."

"If you could be here. . ." She stopped, and then she went on slowly, "Ian, could you come and stay here with me?"

He was taken aback.

"I know how much you love the gatehouse, and your privacy. And the music. But it would only be for a few days. Until I tell her and she goes away."

It wouldn't guarantee her safety, but it would serve as a restraint.

She said, "You could have as much privacy as you want. You don't even have to eat with us if you don't want to. There's a sitting room that goes with the guest room."

"Who knows, just my being here might drive your aunt to leave." She managed a ghost of a smile. "But how would you explain it to your aunt?"

"Do I have to? It's my house. I can invite guests."

"Come now. When she asks you why I'm here, you'll need a reason."

"I could always say it's because . . . the pipes froze in the gatehouse. Nearing always complained about them. I can say you plan to . . . fix them so they won't freeze, but until then you're staying here."

"She won't believe it. But I suppose it isn't that important that she does."

"But you will stay? You're sure you won't mind?"

"I'll feel a lot easier about you if I'm right here with you. Maybe I'd better come over tonight. Would that be inconvenient?"

"Agnes can get the rooms ready in an hour," she said eagerly. "Nearing will move your things over tomorrow, but take what you'll need for tonight. I can even have the television man dismantle your hi-fi and set it up here, if you want. I know how important your music is to you."

"I think I can manage without it for a few days. And, Iris, you did promise to talk to your aunt as soon as you can."

"Yes, I will. And meanwhile, if you want to have friends here, please have them. You can still entertain in the gatehouse, of course. It's yours."

She was thinking of Sally. Better get that settled

once and for all. "I haven't gotten around yet to formal entertaining in the gatehouse," he said. "Sally came, but she came uninvited."

She looked uncomfortable. "I didn't mean Sally, only—"

"I do mean Sally," he said. "Whatever you may hear, or whatever you've seen, I'm not interested in Sally Lucas. I think you were right when you said she came here to hurt you. She certainly doesn't care a hoot about me. Her purpose was to cause embarrassment all around. Forget Sally, if you can, not just because of me, but for your own sake. She's full of hang-ups, but you mustn't let them get to you." He leaned forward. "Do you believe me? About Sally?"

She nodded, as if she at least wanted to believe him.

"Now I'll go home and eat my dinner because it's cooked and I don't want to waste it, and then I'll put my pajamas and toothbrush in my briefcase and get over here."

"I'll ring for Aung Gladys," she said, "And, Ian, I *am* glad you're coming."

He ran down the stairs, only to meet Mrs. Forsher at her door, her face pinched with fury.

"Now you want me out of the house, so you can have your way with her without me there to look after her!"

"Mrs. Forsher, I think you've done a pretty poor job of looking after her."

She caught her breath, and then said harshly, "If you think you can keep what happened between you and Sally Lucas a secret, you've got another think coming.

I'm going to see that Iris knows exactly what goes on!"

"You're wasting your time," he said evenly. "It isn't going to change anything."

She managed a bitter smile. "You'd like to believe that. But I don't give up so easily, and I'm not handing my niece over to you without putting up a fight. If Iris won't believe me, she'll believe Sally, and I'll see to it that she hears Sally's side of it!"

He managed to escape, and went out to his car. The next few days until Iris summoned the courage to speak were going to be tough. He wondered: will she tell her aunt to leave? Does she have the stamina for it?

# 11

*T*he room was somber and smelled musty, since no one had used it in years, maybe not since guests had come at her mother's invitation. Agnes grumbled about opening the windows and letting in the icy wind, but she did air it thoroughly, and dusted. The gardener brought in flowers from the greenhouse, and Iris, who in spite of Dr. Nichols's orders to stay in her room had herself gone down to oversee the preparation of Ian's quarters, arranged bouquets on the mantel and near his bed. A fire was lit, and pine smell filled the room.

She was afraid Sexton would feel obliged to be sociable when he didn't want to, and so she left word with Evans that she had gone to sleep and instructed him to make Dr. Sexton comfortable and serve his breakfast in his room in the morning.

She knew what Aunt Gladys's state of mind would be when she found out about Sexton, and Iris was relieved not to have to see her tonight. But maybe Aunt Gladys would be subdued now; maybe Aunt Gladys would think that if she did not make any fuss, there would be no more talk about the sleeping pills. Ian was right; she did not owe Aunt Gladys anything more. Uncle Bill would increase Aunt Glad's annuity so she could live in comfort, and even go to the Caribbean if she wanted. The important thing was to get her to leave.

*Ralph.* How would she explain it to Ralph without telling him her suspicions about the sleeping pills? The thought appalled her. But just then she heard the doorbell, and the sound of male voices, and then steps coming upstairs. Ian, with Evans. It seemed as if he hesitated as he passed her door. Would he knock? No, of course not. Evans would have told him she was asleep. She heard his laugh as Evans showed him his room, so maybe he was pleased. She pressed her body into her mattress with a shiver of pleasure. He was here, a few yards away from here. It was as if he had put his arms around her and held her and told her everything would be all right from now on.

Iris was awake when Ian left in the morning, and she ran to the window to watch his car drive away. Then she dressed and went downstairs. Aunt Gladys joined her, instead of breakfasting in bed as she often did.

"So you've invited him to stay in the house now."

"Yes, Aunt Gladys."

"I suppose you have your reasons."

"Aunt Gladys, he simply can't heat the house. Nearing always complained, remember, and the other day the pipes froze."

"Isn't that looking a gift horse in the mouth? He was so determined to have the house under any conditions, I thought he would live in it without a roof. So now he's complaining about the heating."

Aunt Gladys was not going to be quelled by anything. Iris sighed. "Aunt Glad, it can be very uncomfortable trying to work in a cold house. You should know. You always like your rooms so very warm." She wished she could get away, and gulped her coffee.

"Iris, Iris, you naïve child. As if Dr. Sexton would let a cold house trouble him. Besides, he's so clever, I'm sure he could improvise something if he wanted to." Aunt Gladys sounded almost gay, trying to pretend she was accepting the situation lightly.

*Aunt Gladys, of course it isn't the heating. Sexton is here because he thinks you tried to kill me, because he thinks you will try again.*

"Wasn't I right after all?" cried Aunt Gladys with the same spurious gaiety. "Didn't he use the gatehouse as a wedge to get himself into the castle? Frozen pipes! He's a sly one, all right. I think he only told you the pipes froze so that you would feel sorry for him and ask him to stay here."

*Aunt Gladys, maybe you would like to go away for a while. Take a trip somewhere. A long cruise, maybe? Go back to New York? You always said how much you missed New York.*

"Oh, well," said Aunt Gladys. "Love is blind. Luckily."

Iris stood up. She had an appointment in Freebody with Dr. Nichols. As she went toward the hall, Aunt Gladys followed her, going on.

"You fell like a ripe plum into his hands, Iris. He knew you would; he knew how sheltered and naïve you are. I'll just stand by and twiddle my thumbs while— Iris, where are you going?"

She was putting on her coat and boots. "Dr. Nichols wants to see me. Just a checkup."

"But why isn't he coming here, the way he always does?"

"I thought I would like to get out."

"All those people in the waiting room?" said Aunt Gladys with odd desperation. "Iris, you know how you hate to go into town."

"I'll be all right, Aunt Glad."

Maybe it was only the knowledge that Sexton was living here that gave her this new confidence. Only once before had she felt so certain that she could face anything, and that was when she had started classes at Freebody, when she thought she had taken her future securely into her own hands. That had failed, but now it was different. Now there was Sexton. She didn't want Sexton to think she was insecure, or neurotic. For him she wanted to be poised and confident, like the other girls he knew. He really didn't think she was neurotic at all; he had assumed at once that she would never try to kill herself, that it had to be someone else.

True, she was despondent that night, but she never wanted to die. She would like to do other things to prove to him that she was just like anybody else. She would like to register for the spring term, for instance. And she wasn't afraid of Sally Lucas anymore. Sexton had assured her that he wasn't interested in Sally.

Wolfe brought the car around. "Sure you wouldn't like me to drive, Miss Freebody?"

"Thanks, Wolfe. I feel like driving myself."

The day sparkled, sun glinting on the fresh, unblemished snow. The plows had cleaned the road, but there were streaks of ice where patches of snow had stayed and melted and then frozen into a solid sheet. She had to drive slowly. Just ahead she saw at least a dozen cars bunched together on the side of the road, and people scattered over the snowy field beyond.

An accident? Those who had stopped had trodden down a portion of red snow-fencing so they could clamber over it more easily, converging on Beaver Pond with its rim of trees. The pond seemed frozen, but here and there water showed blackly through, like inkblots. One of the town's patrol cars was there, and she saw Al Eakins's car, too. Al Eakins was chief of police; he had come to the house to talk to her when Robbie died. He was just getting out of his car as she drove up, and she might have asked him what the trouble was, except she didn't want to remind him of Robbie. She drove on. An ambulance sped past, coming from Concord, racing to Beaver Pond.

A child might have been skating and fallen in. The ice wasn't frozen hard enough, but children were so anxious to skate. . . .

She parked, and went into Dr. Nichols's office. The waiting room was full, but no one seemed to know her. When the nurse called her and asked her name, Iris whispered it so that no one would hear. She was feeling less confident now. She had to steel herself, remind herself that this was what she must do.

"Oh yes, Miss Freebody. Have a chair. It won't be long." The nurse spoke quietly; no one could have heard her. Still, Iris felt people looking at her as she returned to her seat, but that might be only because she was strange to them. She found a magazine and kept her eyes fastened to it.

Two women sat on a sofa near her chair. They had stopped talking briefly when she sat down, but now they resumed their conversation. "No better than she should be," they whispered. "Imagine, a child of fourteen . . . But then, what could you expect, raised by her sister . . . No time to watch her . . . Little ones of her own . . . I heard . . ." The voices dropped. ". . . even the husband and Sally . . ."

Iris stiffened, clutching the magazine which almost slipped from her lap.

"No good end, you might guess . . ." the voices went on, strophe and antistrophe. "Still . . . college, the first of her family to reach college . . . and that's for sure . . . drunk, but then a girl in a bar . . . she was a waitress, I heard. Still . . . there *was* a bar . . . half the men in town . . . I heard she was alone."

She lifted her terrified eyes as the nurse called her name. She wanted to bolt, but it was too late; the nurse was waiting for her, looking at her as if she were odd not to come forward at once. So she made her leaden legs carry her to the book-lined and antiseptic safety of Dr. Nichols's office.

"What's the matter with you, Iris?" Dr. Nichols said sharply.

"I just heard . . . Did something happen . . . to   ."

"Sally Lucas," the doctor said shortly. "Who told you? Is it on the radio already?"

"Some women in the waiting room," she whispered. "I heard them talking, and the name Sally."

"They found her this morning, early," Dr. Nichols said. "Forget it, Iris. Don't think about such things. It isn't any of your business."

"I want to know," she said. "I'll find out anyway, in the papers. What happened?"

"They found her car empty alongside the road—"

"The road leading past our house," she said. "I drove on it just now and I saw the police, and the ambulance."

"Yes, well, there was no one in the car, but the snow was trampled, and someone took the trouble to follow the trail. She was drowned, I imagine."

"But how?"

"She may have been drunk, lost her head, lost her way—it's only speculation, and they haven't finished examining the body yet, so it's too soon to tell. Iris, it's unfortunate. It's sad. It's ugly. But you have to put it out of your mind. Now let's have a look at you. How are you feeling?"

She was fine, the examination proved. Yet Dr. Nichols was worried about the state of her nerves and only reluctantly consented to let her go her way.

172

"I can drop you off later, when I start making calls. Or my nurse can drive you. Or a cab—"

"I can drive, thanks," she said.

She went through the waiting room without glancing to either side, and found her car and drove home. There were still cars at the place where Sally had died, curious spectators, and the snow was trampled beyond the skill of any detective to decipher. Still, someone had seen it first, someone could tell if there were footprints, if they were a man's or a woman's, or more than one set.

Aunt Gladys was talking to Evans in the hall when she came in. They both looked up when they saw her, and fell silent. Evans left and Aunt Gladys said, "Have you heard?"

Iris nodded. "I saw the place on the road. I had to pass it. And Dr. Nichols told me."

"It was on the TV already, from White River Junction," Aunt Gladys said. "They said she worked late at the café, and had been drinking with one of the men there, but that she left alone. Of course, she might have met someone afterward. A girl like that. Still, even if she got what she deserved, she was such a young girl, only nineteen. Who could have wanted her dead?"

Iris waited for Ian to come home. He stayed in his room a long time after he returned, and she waited anxiously for a sound to indicate that he might be coming out. Finally she had to go down to dinner, and she stopped at his door and tapped.

He opened it abruptly, his face clearing a little when

he saw her. "Iris? Feeling all better?"

She nodded. "Will you have dinner with us? You can have it alone if you prefer. I'll tell Agnes."

"Dinner?" He seemed to have forgotten. "Yes, well. . ." He thought. "I'll have it with you if I may."

She found herself letting out her breath. She had been afraid he would stay in his room and there would be no chance to talk to him about Sally. And she had to talk to him, she had to see his face when they talked about her, she had to know how much it mattered to him.

"Wait here," he said. "I'll get my jacket and we'll go down together." He went to the closet. "I suppose you know by now."

"Yes. I was on my way to Dr. Nichols this morning and I saw all the cars. They were talking about it in the office when I got there."

She thought he would say something more, but he didn't. His face was grim, and he seemed deep in his own thoughts. He was disturbed by Sally's death, then, but any more than she? Was there something else?

Aunt Gladys was waiting in the dining room when they came down. She seemed surprised to see him, but managed to nod her head in the most formal of acknowledgments, and asked Agnes to set another place.

"I think we'll have some wine," said Iris remembering belatedly that Sexton liked wine with his dinner. "Agnes, will you tell Evans to bring a bottle?"

"What are they saying in town, Dr. Sexton?" Aunt Gladys said as they sat down. "About Sally? People in town know things that even the police don't find out."

"There's a lot of talk, of course, in school. She was a student, so it's natural. But no one seems to know anything. It's conjecture, mostly. The medical report says death by drowning."

"Someone could have held her head in the water," Aunt Gladys said. "The announcer said that with her coat collar and muffler protecting her, someone could have put his hands on her neck and held her down until she drowned, and there would be no marks to show it."

"It could have happened that way," Ian said. "I understand there were no clear footprints. It was as if she had staggered and fallen in the snow several times, obliterating the prints."

"The announcer said she could have been dragged, and that's why there were no clear prints."

"Will you have some more wine, Aunt Gladys?"

"Yes, thanks, angel."

"Ian?"

He shook his head. "It's possible that she was drunk. One of the students saw her at the café after she was through with her job, and she was drinking with one of the men there. He left before she did, and everyone seemed to think she left the bar alone. It's possible that she was unable to drive, and stopped the car, and felt sick, and got out. She could have lost her bearings and wandered off to the pond instead of back to her car."

"How could she get her head underwater when the pond was frozen solid?" Aunt Gladys cried.

He said evenly, "It wasn't frozen solid. They had

posted a 'No Skating' sign on it. There were some parts that were frozen, at the very edges, but it was thin or broken within a few feet."

There was a pause. Then Aunt Gladys said, "That would make it very simple for anyone who had it in for her."

Sexton said nothing.

Aunt Glady's mouth tightened. "I'd like a little more wine, Iris. Why don't we have wine more often? Ralph insists on it when he's here, but then that boy has learned how to live like a gentleman at Harvard."

Iris thought Aunt Gladys was finished with Sally's death, but it seemed she wasn't. Her face was suffused with color, and she seemed to have difficulty enunciating her words.

"No, there's more to it than meets the eye, Dr. Sexton. When a girl like that dies in a mysterious way, you can bet there's more to it than meets the eye."

"Aunt Glad sees too many daytime serials."

"Don't say it like that, Iris. People make fun of them, but there's a lot that's true-to-life in them. You can't guess what's in people's hearts just by appearances. There was this episode a few months ago about a boy who was going to marry this dreadful girl. A cheap tramp, that's all she was, but the boy couldn't see the truth, no matter what his mother said, or how she warned him against her. Would have ruined his whole life, she would have. He was going in for the diplomatic corps, and you can imagine how far he would have gotten with those refined diplomats and their wives, married to a tramp like that. His mother knew. She'd sacrificed to send him through college, and buy him good clothes, and give him enough money so he could mix with the right people. You couldn't blame her for not wanting to see it go down the drain. Pushed that girl right out the window, she did. Nobody knows. They think it was an accident. The hinge on the French door was loose. She loosened it a little more, and everybody thinks the girl leaned on it and it gave—"

She stopped, her face flat and pasty.

"That was clever," Ian said. "Shows what lengths even loving mothers will be driven to, pressed hard enough."

"I don't know what you mean," Aunt Gladys said thickly. "There's plenty going on here that won't bear looking into, as far as that goes. I could be just as sly, hinting plenty—"

"Aunt Gladys, maybe you should go and lie down. You're not used to so much wine." She went over to her aunt's chair and tried to coax her to her feet. "Would you like to go up to your room, or would you like to lie down in your sitting room?"

Aunt Gladys struggled in her grasp, and turned to point a finger at Sexton. "Mind you, Sally Lucas was killed in the nick of time, before she could talk! And she was shut up only because someone knew she could make trouble for him! I wouldn't be at all surprised if she was going to have a baby. Nice story that would make, if they find out she's pregnant. And I have some ideas on that, if anyone asks me!"

Iris led Aunt Gladys toward the sitting room because she knew she could never manage to get her up the stairs. She made her comfortable with a pillow, and turned on the TV for her.

"Is there anything else you want, Aunt Gladys?"

"Just find me my cigarettes," Aunt Gladys mumbled. "They're under that cushion there. And the ashtray."

Iris put them within her reach.

"Iris, you watch out for that man," Aunt Gladys said thickly. "He's cleared the way for himself. Nothing can stop him."

Iris left her, closing the door behind her. Ian was standing in the hall, watching her when she came out. Had he heard Aunt Gladys's words? He looked worn, and grim. She did not want to be alone, and she was afraid he would go up to his room and get to his work. She said quickly, "Could we have a lesson?"

He was disconcerted, as if a lesson were the last thing on his mind. He frowned, and then he said, "Do you feel up to it? No reactions from the pills?"

"No reactions at all," she assured him eagerly. "It could be short, if you have work to do. I did say I wouldn't interfere with your work, Ian, and I won't."

He smiled and shrugged. "You're not interfering. I'm not in any mood for work, myself. But let's read a little. That's hardly work."

She ran up ahead of him to light the lamps and get out her books.

When he came into her room he was in his old flannel shirt, his feet in moccasins, his book under his arm.

178

"I don't even have to go out in the cold to get here," he said, settling himself into his usual chair.

She thought, now it will be the way it was before, the utter happiness she felt when she was with him. But almost before they were under way there was a knock on the door.

It was Evans. "Excuse me, Miss Freebody, but there's a telephone call for Dr. Sexton."

He stood up. "I'll take it in my room."

She had a sudden and overwhelming feeling of foreboding. She continued to sit in her chair, waiting, until he came back. But when he came from his room he was dressed to go out, in his mackinaw and boots.

"I have to go into town, Iris. I won't be long, but we might as well give up on the lesson for tonight."

"What. . .?" But she didn't want to pry; she had promised him his privacy. She shut her lips over the unasked question. And he pretended he didn't know it was on her lips. He said only, "Good night," and ran down the stairs before she could weaken.

She stood leaning through the columns and fretted stone of the minstrel gallery, watching the front door close quickly behind him, feeling suddenly alone, and vulnerable.

Someone moved in the shadows. She started violently, but it was only Coffey. Coffey drew her back with her into her room and carefully closed the door.

"Honestly, Coffey, you did scare me."

"I didn't want her to hear us talking. Dr. Sexton says I must be careful, do you know that? He says if she thinks I'm on to her, she'll try to get rid of me some-

179

how, and then who will look out for you? He says I'm to lock my door at night, do you know that?"

"Maybe you should do what he says, Coffey."

"I am. I only came out now because I had to tell you something. I waited until she shut herself up in there. Dead to the world, isn't she? She must have been at the bottle, the way she's snoring."

"Oh, Coffey, she had a few glasses of wine. She isn't used to it, that's all."

"You can hear her sawing away louder than she blasts those infernal programs. I was just down there. That's how I knew it was safe to talk. Listen, Iris, you know where Dr. Sexton went just now?"

Iris's heart began to beat very fast. "No. And don't tell me."

"Don't be a child, Iris. You'll know sooner or later. That was Al Eakins, called him down to the police station. About Sally Lucas."

Iris drew a deep breath. "I suppose they'll be calling down everybody who knew her, and Sally was in his class. They'll want to know if he can help with any information."

"Iris, they're going to find out about him and Sally. I wouldn't say it, except it's got to come out now."

"There was nothing between him and Sally, Coffey. She liked him and she hung around him, that was all. He isn't interested in her."

Coffey said, "That's not what *she* told the police. She called this afternoon and I listened in."

She found her voice. "Aunt Gladys called the police?"

"She told them about Sally, and him. Maybe it isn't true, and maybe she's lying, but what she told the police was that Sally would come to his house nights. The police department could take it from there. That's why they've sent for him, I think, to ask him about her."

Iris thought for only a moment. He might deny it, and then they would know he was lying, which would reinforce their suspicions.

"I must catch him before he leaves!" She ran downstairs, snatched her coat from the closet and pulled it on as she let herself out. Belatedly, anger surged up in her against Aunt Gladys. How dare she phone the police! But then, she was learning at last that Aunt Gladys would stop at nothing.

Below at the entrance gates she saw Sexton's car poised in front of the gates, waiting for them to open.

"Dr. Sexton!"

She froze. Someone else was hurrying toward Sexton's car, Nearing's short, heavy-set figure, calling out to Sexton. She crept back into the shadow of the shrubs, moving closer, but unseen.

Sexton cut his motor, waiting.

Nearing reached the car and stood there. His voice was harshly audible.

"Evans told us the police want to talk to you about Sally."

Sexton answered him, but she couldn't make out what he said.

Nearing said, "I've got nothing to hide any more'n you have. I've made a good name for myself all these years, and I don't want anything to do with the police. They'll drag my boy's name in it sure as you're born, and I don't want that muck stirred up again. I want him to lie in his grave in peace."

She almost stopped breathing in order to hear Sexton's reply, but it was still inaudible.

Nearing spoke again. "If you keep quiet about that night in the gatehouse, I give you my word I won't tell them she was there with you, and what I saw. And that's my word."

This time the blood pulsed deafeningly in her ears; she did not know if Ian replied at all. But the gates were opening, and Ian was driving through. Nearing clumped back up the drive, and she remained pressed into the bushes until he was out of sight and the gates closed again.

Ian had lied; there *had* been something between them. The only one who knew, besides Sally who was dead, was Nearing. Nearing would barter his silence for Ian's, so Sexton was safe.

No. Aunt Gladys knew. She had phoned the police and probably told them. And Sexton knew she knew.

# *12*

$S$ he lay awake, listening for Sexton to come home. Suppose they found evidence which would seem to involve him. Would they keep him at the police station? But just on suspicion? Just because he had known her? Even . . . made love to her? What about the other men who had known her, and loved her? The man in the café that night, what about him? Anyway, why should it be anything but an accident? As Sexton said, Sally might have stopped her car to be sick, and wandered toward the pond instead of back to her car, mistaken the edge for solid ground because of the snow covering it, and fallen in, too stupefied to know what was happening to her. Why did it have to be murder? And if it was, why should Sexton even be considered a suspect? He wasn't the murderer type—too disciplined, too intelligent, too reasonable. . . .

At last she heard the sound of his car on the drive. She waited, giving him time to put his car in the garage and make his way to the front door. She knew how long it should take; she had counted these minutes often. And now she heard the front door open. Throwing on a robe, she opened her bedroom door to catch him before he went past into his room.

He did not come past. There was just the faint sound of another door shutting. The pantry? Had he gone looking for something to eat? Maybe he had gone out again to get something from the car that he had forgotten. But the sound of the front door latch was unmistakable; she would have heard that if he had opened it. And she did not hear even the faintest sound of footsteps; even if he were walking carefully, she should have heard footsteps.

The hall was in darkness. Ever since the power shortage, they had begun to turn out unnecessary lights, and since the switch was just inside the front door, anyone coming home would be able to light his way to the stairs. She waited; she could have been mistaken. She was so anxious to see him return she might almost have imagined it. The sound of his motor? The latch sliding heavily into place? She could have been wrong—

She suppressed a cry. He appeared in front of her, in the faint light reflected from her windows.

"Iris!"

He seemed as startled as she was.

"Are you still up?" he said, collecting himself with an effort that was audible in his voice. He was trying to appear at ease, but he was plainly upset.

"I heard you come in," she whispered. "I . . . just wanted . . . to know if everything is all right."

"Everything is fine," he said. "Iris, I'm very tired. If you don't mind, I'll turn in now."

"Of course," she said, embarrassed. "I didn't realize . . ."

His door closed behind him.

He had seemed very disturbed. Something had happened, something he didn't want to talk about. He had been disconcerted at seeing her. He had come upstairs quietly so as not to wake anybody, and he had been upset when she had seen him. No, she was using her imagination now, building on a few chance words —*I won't say what I saw, if you keep quiet*—Nearing's words. What had Nearing seen? Suddenly she shivered, feeling as if there were an evil fate stalking her, dooming whoever came close to her. . .

She caught herself sharply. What evil fate? What doom? She must not allow herself to be neurotic; she must be sane and clear and sensible, like Sexton. She must not allow herself ever again to be the frightened, cowering girl she had been before Ian, for her own sake more than his. But for his, too. What would he think of her? Why should he be interested in a girl he would have to tend like a nurse all her life? *If* there was any hope of their living together someday. She swallowed, and resolutely made herself stop thinking of Sally Lucas.

She got into bed, and even slept, but fitfully. She dreamed of Sally, and her face now in death looking the way Robbie's had looked. . . . And then it was Robbie she saw again, his sneakered feet dangling so childishly, with the rip near the big toe and the scab on his gray-white ankle. The gatehouse was burning, flames were shooting up, destroying it, the beautiful gatehouse Sexton had built, all going up in clouds of smoke—

She wrenched her eyes open in anguish. Dawn was gray, and a gray, furry mist lay over the valley beyond the windows. Smoke. She smelled smoke. A fireplace? Aunt Glad's cigarettes? Could she be smoking so early in the morning? No, the smell was too strong. She pulled on her robe and opened her front door. The hall below was full of smoke.

She ran to Sexton's door and pounded on it. "Ian!"

It seemed forever before he opened his door and stared at her in confusion.

"I think the house is on fire!"

"The phone. I'll get the Fire Department!"

She heard him shouting into the telephone as she ran downstairs. Coffey! And Evans! And Agnes! Aunt Glad! She started blindly back up the stairs and collided with someone.

Coffey.

"Coffey! You're all right? I was afraid . . . Coffey, come here with me!" She dragged her down the last of the stairs and across the hall to the front door, unbolting it with feverish haste and flinging it wide open. "Stay there! So if you have to get out . . . I have to wake the others."

But Agnes materialized out of the smoke, coming from the back where the servants' staircase was. Evans followed her. They were all safe then. Wolfe and

Nearing slept over the garage. Cook went home nights. Aunt Glad!

As she started back up she met Sexton coming down. "Aunt Gladys! She sleeps so soundly—"

"She isn't in her room," he said briefly. "I looked." He propelled her toward the door where the servants stood. Agnes had put a blanket around Coffey's shoulders. "Stay here," he told Iris. "I'll look around."

She leaned against the door. Now she knew what must have happened. Aunt Gladys had set the house on fire. She hated them all enough to want to burn the house down around them. She had gone mad with desperation, had been willing to see the house destroyed with Iris in it rather than allow her to share it with Sexton. And then she had run away.

She saw Sexton cross to the sitting room and open the door. A dense cloud of acrid smoke billowed out. As she stood immobilized with horror, she saw him disappear inside. The sofa where Aunt Gladys always lay was a black pyre, lit weirdly by small tongues of flame licking around the cushions. Something lay on the sofa, blackened by smoke, a single tongue of fire shining behind her smoking hair.

Someone was screaming. She? Sexton had grasped the smoke-blackened shape and was dragging it out into the hall. Nearing had come in, and Wolfe. One of them flung a rug over the figure, but there were no flames to extinguish. Someone was in the sitting room, opening windows. Smoke still emerged from the shape under the rug, and the terrible smell filled her nostrils.

Sirens sounded, and engines crunched on the icy gravel of the driveway. There were other voices raised now, and people milling about. Someone drew her away, and when she couldn't make her feet move, she was lifted, and carried upstairs.

Sexton's face hung over her, grimy, his eyes tired. She felt his hand touch her face, her hair, and then he disappeared. When she looked for him, she saw Dr. Nichols instead. She struggled to sit up. "Ian!"

"He's here. Everyone is okay. You lie down and let me give you something to make you sleep." She saw the network of lines and creases in his face enlarged beyond reality as a needle pierced her arm.

"Aunt Gladys! I mustn't sleep!"

"You must. Time to talk later," Dr. Nichols said.

Dimly she heard the voices shouting downstairs, and things crashing down. They were destroying the Castle. Let them. Let it burn. It was an evil house, where evil things happened. Why hadn't she burned instead of Aunt Gladys? It was she who destroyed everybody that touched her. She should have burned and died, not Aunt Gladys.

# 13

*L*ater that day Iris came downstairs to answer Chief Eakins's questions. Dr. Nichols had sedated her heavily early that morning, but the sedative had worn off, and when she heard the police chief's car she insisted on coming down.

She sat with her hands clasped so tightly the knuckles showed white, and said that she didn't know anything until the smell of smoke must have waked her, that she thought it was then past six because the sky was gray, that she had run to wake Dr. Sexton, and he had called the Fire Department. Yes, it was Dr. Sexton who had opened the sitting-room door and discovered her aunt's body.

She did not mention meeting him at her bedroom door in the early hours of the morning when he had come back from the police station. Maybe she found it embarrassing to admit that she had been waiting up for him. And so when it was his turn to answer questions, he said nothing about seeing Iris then either.

Iris stayed while he spoke to Eakins. Eakins knew Ian had spent the last two nights in her house because, as both Iris and Ian explained, the pipes were frozen in the gatehouse.

Eakins said, "Near as I can remember, Dr. Sexton, you left for home after midnight."

Ian nodded.

"Go straight home?"

He nodded again.

"And you didn't smell smoke when you came in? The fire fellows say it must have been smoldering for hours. You should have noticed it, if it had started by then."

Ian shook his head. "Matter of fact, I stayed downstairs for about fifteen minutes after I got back. I knew Miss Freebody wouldn't mind if I raided the refrigerator. If there had been smoke, I would have noticed it. But of course the door was shut tight."

Iris's eyes rested on him. Her gaze was remote, and oddly blank, but he blamed that on the shock and the heavy sedation. He thought it would be good for her if he could get her to talk, and he waited impatiently for Eakins to leave. But she did not give him a chance.

As soon as the door closed behind the police chief she said quietly, "I think you should go back to the gatehouse now. Dr. Nichols phoned for Ralph, and he'll be here by evening. I'd rather he didn't know you've been sleeping here these last two nights, and though he may find out anyway, he's less likely to if you're gone when he comes."

She's in shock, he reminded himself. He wanted to

take her for a walk in the cold, clean air and tell her that it had been no one's fault, what happened; that her aunt had probably fallen asleep after all that wine and not even known it when her cigarette smoldered in the cushions; that she probably did not even know it when she died. He couldn't say that her death had been tragic, but just. She was a murderer in intent, even if she had failed, and her death was in its way retribution, but he couldn't say that, either.

She turned away from him before he could try and speak.

So Nearing moved him back to the gatehouse. He had brought very little. When he went to the door with Nearing, Ian tipped him for his trouble. He said, "You asked me to be discreet last night, and I was. Now I'll ask the same favor of you. Miss Freebody doesn't want Mr. Forsher to know that I stayed in the house for the last two nights."

He expected a leer and a wink, at least, but Nearing barely lifted his head. His face looked gray, his eyes rheumy, and he hardly seemed to hear.

Ian said, "The police know I was there, so it isn't a question of concealing evidence, and it's very likely he'll find out somehow anyway. But you might mention to the servants not to say anything, that Miss Freebody prefers it that way."

Nearing went off, head bent deep in his shoulders. Over Mrs. Forsher's death? No, it was Sally Lucas. Of course. The aunt's death had wiped the other from his own mind, but for Nearing, Sally's death must be the reopening of a deep-seated wound.

The gatehouse seemed unfamiliar, and indefinably altered. It was as if it had lost its first innocence for him. Or maybe it was he who had lost it, that sense of a fresh new beginning, of the future spreading wide and full of hope before him, glowing with promise. It was as if the old stain of Robbie's death had reappeared after weeks of scouring and polishing. He was restless, and wished he could confront Iris. Maybe he could just check in and see how she was; maybe the sedative would have worn off by now, and some of the shock, and things would be as they were. He should leave her alone tonight. But instead he went back up to the house to see her anyway.

She was in her room when he rang the bell, and instead of asking him to come up as she always did, she said he was to wait in the living room.

There were sounds of activity behind the smoke-grimed door to the sitting room.

"Are they cleaning up already?" he asked, surprised. He'd understood from Eakins that everything was to stay as it was until the coroner's report was in from Concord where Mrs. Forsher's body had been taken.

Evans nodded. "The police called Mr. Tieman, Miss Freebody's lawyer, and he came here for dinner. He just left a little while ago, and he told us it would be all right to have the decorator from town straighten up. People will be arriving for the funeral, and we would like no sign of . . ." He stopped, embarrassed, as if it could be construed as unseemly haste.

"Better for Miss Freebody, to do away with any reminder," Ian said.

192

Evans said, his voice lower, "We're all surprised here that it didn't happen sooner. That sofa had just been reupholstered because of all the cigarette burns. Mrs. Forsher would fall asleep in front of the TV, and her cigarette would slip out of the ashtray. If she hadn't had too much wine last night, she would have waked up before it happened."

So the household knew about the wine, too. Agnes must have mentioned it, and how Iris practically had to carry her aunt to the sitting room after dinner.

He grew uneasy waiting for Iris, wondering if she were delaying coming down on purpose, though what purpose he couldn't imagine. But finally she appeared in the doorway, tall and very pale in a dark dress.

She said, "You shouldn't have come. Ralph is just driving in."

Because he was hurt, he said bluntly, "Is there any reason he shouldn't see us together?"

"I don't want him to see you, or talk to you. I don't want to give him any reason to suspect, to ask questions, and find out that you were staying here. If he finds out, he'll want to know why, and I won't convince him of the frozen pipes. I don't want him to guess about Aunt Gladys, ever. Ever!" Her eyes reddened with tears.

"I'll leave at once," he said. "Shall I use the back door?"

She swallowed, fighting for self-control, and then turned hastily away from him, running out into the hall where Evans was opening the front door.

Ralph came in, and she flung herself into his arms,

allowing herself to cry without restraint. Ralph's face over her shoulder looked haggard and bewildered. Together, their arms around each other, they went upstairs.

Ian came out of the living room and let himself out.

He built himself a beautiful fire in the gatehouse and tried to draw some warmth from it. That night he had come back from the police, she had been waiting for him, anxious about him. "I wouldn't care if you were a fortune hunter," she had said, "if it were the only way. . . ." He repeated her words, he thought of the way she always looked when she saw him, he remembered her kiss that cold night in the snow, and her mouth open to his as if she could not bring him close enough.

She had made her feelings plain from the beginning, like the naïve, inexperienced girl she was. It was he who had held back, it was he who had been afraid of the brush-fire quality of her emotions.

Then why did he let it get him this way?

It was simply that he wanted to understand her, and couldn't. Unless she was so neurotic that she could turn her emotions on and off for any reason . . . No. She was not neurotic. She was shy, and sensitive, and afraid of the world with good reason. And one of the reasons she had liked him was that she knew he saw her this way. He had thought of her as capable of discerning between love and need, and she had proved to him that she could.

Only . . . this didn't make sense.

\*     \*     \*

194

He stayed away from the house the next day, and at night as well, even though the house was lit from top to bottom and a steady stream of cars kept coming up the drive so that Nearing finally left the gates open. She'd said she had no family, but Ralph did, and many of the cars belonged to Ralph's family, he supposed, and Ralph's friends. And there were people from the town who knew Mrs. Forsher; she did attend church, and write checks from Iris for various organizations in Freebody, and there were tradespeople who no doubt had padded their bills and split them with her, and thus would miss her. He had the wry feeling that many of these people were there to get inside the Freebody gates and see Iris Freebody and her life-style rather than because of any real regret over her aunt. Mrs. Forsher was hardly the kind of woman to inspire even pity, let alone regret.

However, he did go to the church for the funeral services. He stayed in back, away from Iris, until later when the services were over and people were talking in knots on the sidewalk, and Iris was momentarily alone.

He went over to her. "Is there anything I can do?"

Her eyes looked through him. She shook her head without replying. At that moment her car drew up, and she went to it and got in without a backward glance. Ralph appeared suddenly, glanced at Ian quickly and then away again, obviously hoping not to have to acknowledge him. But that brief meeting of eyes gave Ian a chance to follow through on the civilities. He went up to Ralph before the younger man could follow Iris into the car, and offered his hand. "Sorry about your mother—"

"Thanks," Ralph said without waiting for him to finish. The glance he shot back, though, was disturbingly familiar; it held the same hatred his mother had revealed.

Ian watched them drive away to the cemetary, then got into his car and went home.

Home. It had stopped feeling like home. Odd, but in the beginning, when there was only the parent-teacher or helpful-friend-to-troubled-young-woman relationship between him and Iris, he hadn't needed her warmth to make the gatehouse home. In fact, in the beginning her instant response to him had been somewhat onerous, as if he had had other things to cope with before he could take on any more involvement. Now the house seemed arid, devoid of any real interest. He walked around moodily, and then got a can of stain and some rags and went to work on the kitchen shelves, which he had decided he might leave unfinished. He found the work did not distract him, and he kept listening for a knock on his door, or a message from the house.

Maybe she wanted Ralph to leave first. Maybe she thought it would be heaping injury upon injury for Ralph to see them together. He thought of the way she had rushed into Ralph's arms the night of Ralph's arrival. Pity? Pity only?

Damn it, he could just see her going back to Ralph, marrying him as an act of atonement for those unjustified feelings of guilt.

Damn it, he hadn't even wanted her! He had wanted her so little that even the thought of her fortune hadn't convinced him that he should reach out his hand for it and take it, and her. He was the one who had held back. He'd felt sorry for her, that was all, and then he had been angered by the way that aunt and her son had locked her in their coils, and then he had been enraged by the cold-blooded attempts on her life that she wouldn't even acknowledge as genuine threats.

That didn't add up to love.

Let her marry Ralph, if she had to. Ralph would probably kick him out of the gatehouse, once he was in command. Let him. It was just a house. He'd find a room in town for the rest of the year. He might go back to New York when the year was up, anyway. This experience hadn't been a total loss, at least. When she had waked him the other night and he had smelled smoke, at first he had thought it was the old nightmare, wrapped up with Frannie. He had thought, I can't look at her, I can't touch her. But he had. He had looked at her and touched her and grabbed her dead feet and pulled her out, and now he did not think he would dream of Frannie anymore. Thank you for that much, Miss Freebody, he thought bitterly, and then was surprised to find himself trembling.

# *14*

All day she would walk up and down in her room making plans. At night she lay awake for hours, making plans. The trouble was she did not think she could carry them out. That took clear thinking, and courage, and she couldn't summon up either. She did not go out much at all, except when she knew Ian was at school. She was afraid she would meet him, and she knew it was important that she not see him anymore. The first week after the funeral he had called and asked to see her, but she had told Evans she would see no one, and when he called she would lock her door in case he was angry enough to brush past Evans and come upstairs anyway. But he didn't, and it had been days since he had come. Better this way.

She had ordered the county newspaper to be delivered along with the *Freebody Monitor*. As soon as she heard the truck come with the newspapers she would listen, waiting for Evans to put them on the living-room table and go away, because she didn't want him to notice her eagerness to read the papers, and wonder about her sudden interest. And then she would steal down and take them back to her room.

There was nothing about Aunt Gladys, after the story covering her death. She had died from asphyxiation due to smoke inhalation, the newspaper report had said, and they had headlined it: PROMINENT RESIDENT OF FREEBODY DIES IN HER SLEEP, as if to play down the horror. There was a formal notice of the funeral, and a few days later a discreet editorial about the dangers of falling asleep while smoking. But they didn't go so far as to mention Aunt Gladys by name.

Even Sally Lucas's name was disappearing from the papers. There would be an interview now and then with Chief Eakins, but the conclusion seemed to be they had no positive evidence of foul play. One day there was a banner headline that the man had been found, the one with whom Sally had spent her last night at the café. He had come forward to be questioned. But even that turned out to be nothing. He had never even spoken to Sally before that night, and afterward he left her to catch a bus; he had gone on to Manchester where his girl lived.

The man was a traveling representative for a water-softening firm and since he constantly moved from town to town, didn't always catch up with the local news. The bus driver confirmed his story, and, after all, what motive could a stranger have for killing Sally?

What motive could Ian have, for that matter—just because she came to his house, even if she slept with him? He wouldn't be stupid enough to kill her so she couldn't tell Iris there was anything between them. Not Sexton; he was too intelligent for that, wasn't he?

What did the police do when they reached an impasse? They had called it accidental death, but had they left the case open in the event of new evidence? She brooded. Freebody didn't have a force of detectives. Al Eakins was chief of police and a detective, too. In fact, there wouldn't even be the two patrol cars if there hadn't been a brief riot in the college over the firing of someone on the faculty. Had Sally been a prominent citizen, Al Eakins might have referred the case to the county. But Sally's sister and the sister's husband were satisfied with the verdict of accidental death. Maybe they wanted to avoid what might be raked up.

Ralph was afraid she was in danger. On his last weekend at the Castle he said, "Maybe it would be the best thing if we got married and you came to live with me in Cambridge while I finished school."

She hid her dismay at the idea. "I couldn't *now*, Ralph. How could I? I mean, so soon after . . . I just couldn't."

Gloomily, he had to agree with her.

"And anyway, why should I be in danger, Ralph, any more than before?"

"Because there were two deaths in town within a week of each other," he said. "Freebody never had a

200

murder for as long as I can remember. Maybe there's a sick killer on the loose."

"Your mother wasn't murdered. And the police think Sally Lucas's death was an accident, too."

"That's what they say. Makes it convenient for them not to have to spend the time and money on an investigation. It's lucky for everyone that no one gives a damn why Sally died. Everyone expected something like this to happen to her, and a lot of people think she only got what she deserved."

Her throat was dry. "But you haven't any reason to say it was anything but an accident."

"They never gave any publicity to the fact that her face was bashed in. They said it had rubbed against the frozen roots in the water—" He stopped when he saw her expression. "I won't talk about it anymore. I'm sorry, Iris."

Her nausea passed. "You can't think that because Sally may have been killed, Aunt Gladys was."

"I'm not at all satisfied that my mother's death was an accident," he said grimly. "I don't want any notoriety to fall on the family if it can be avoided. You've had plenty in the past, and now that I'm being considered by a law firm as conservative as Hayworth, Stanley and Green, it might be disastrous. But I'm not finished with it by any means, and as soon as I get some spare time I'm going to do a little investigating on my own."

"What will you investigate?" she said faintly.

"I have a couple of hunches." He kissed her goodbye. "Iris, you have to be very careful. I've already instructed Nearing to get on the ball. Remember, the killer may be smooth and shrewd, and wily, and his strength lies in the fact that he doesn't seem or look like a killer. Promise me you won't trust anybody. *Anybody.*"

She promised. She clung to him at the door with a rush of tenderness and pity for him. He had no one but her now. And in a way, she had no one but him.

He promised to be back to spend Christmas with her. She watched him drive away. Did he blame her for his mother's death, and was he hiding the accusation from her? Who was there for him to investigate, except Ian?

She told herself there was no such thing as a curse, or an evil fate. She allowed herself to think in those terms only when she was frightened and overwrought, but she knew rationally that such concepts were nonsense.

I must be practical, and realistic, she told herself, and being practical and realistic meant recognizing that people hungered for money and sex, lost their heads over money and sex, died to possess them, killed to possess them. The kidnapper had been destroyed by her money. Robbie had been destroyed by her money. Even Aunt Gladys had, in a way—because if she hadn't stayed in the hopes of possessing some of it, she might have lived out her life happily in New York or somewhere.

To someone who had never had any money at all, so much money had to seem dazzling, mind-boggling. If

Aunt Gladys had been clever, and not driven to distraction by her fear of losing what she had begun to believe was hers, she might have taken the time to find out what constituted a lethal dose of sleeping pills. In her anxiety to be sure, she had put in too many, which was what had made her vomit them up at once. If Aunt Gladys had been more calculating, it would be she who was dead, not Aunt Gladys.

But Sexton was on to her. Sexton knew that Aunt Gladys was dangerous not only to her, but to him. He knew Aunt Gladys had told the police about Sally's visits to the gatehouse, but he still didn't know if Aunt Gladys had told *her*. And that might be important to him, if he loved her. Could he love her? Was it only her money, again? Was her money important to Ian? Somehow, she could not believe it.

But then, she could not believe he was a murderer, either. Suppose, though, he was hard-driven; suppose Sally Lucas had threatened to expose him, disgrace him, cause him to lose his job, maybe cast a shadow on his whole academic future. Suppose it was a combination of all of these. Didn't everyone have a breaking point, beyond which he might do something that wasn't in him to do?

Not Sexton.

*She* was the nub of all this tragedy, she and her wealth. But there was still time to save Sexton, avert suspicion from him. She must send him away. He must leave the gatehouse. Nobody would suspect him of having a motive for killing if he were to go away and she were never to see him again. There would be no talk. More important, there would be no investigation by Ralph. Ralph would lose interest in Sexton if he did not think she cared about him.

She brooded. She thought some more. But if she turned him out of the gatehouse now, wouldn't *that* cast a cloud of suspicion on him? Wouldn't people wonder if she herself suspected he'd had a part in Sally's death, maybe in Aunt Gladys's, too? Wouldn't they say that Iris Freebody did not want a murder suspect on her premises?

There was only one way to resolve the situation, and the sleepless hours and the waking thoughts finally reached the solution. She must go away herself.

Once her decision was made, she acted quickly, before she could allow her fears to overwhelm her. In the morning she asked Wolfe to bring around her father's little car, explaining that she wanted to drive to Concord to see Bill Tieman. But she had no intention of seeing Bill Teiman—then. Down the street from his office was a travel agency. She remembered it, and she would go there to make her plans final.

Coffey hovered over her that morning almost as if she suspected. Coffey had diminished since Aunt Gladys's death; her hatred of Aunt Gladys had suffused her with an odd vitality and energy. Now she was deflated, shrunken, terribly frail. Her hand, like a shriveled claw, held aside the drapes, watching the car move away.

When she entered the travel agency, the clerk behind the counter was busy on the phone, and she wandered around, looking at the posters showing the beauties of Europe. Yes, she would go to Europe; of that much she was certain. It would be too easy for someone to follow her if she stayed in the States. In Europe she could get lost. Besides, it was in the tradition. Freebody women invariably sought escape from Freebody by going to Europe. If people in town talked about her abrupt departure, they would be bound to follow it up with: "Just like her mother. Her mother was always taking herself off to France."

France. She would go to France. Almost as if her eyes had been guided, she was staring at the poster on the wall. A stone-rimmed harbor, a cobbled street, half-timbered houses, the masts of fishing boats . . . She bent close to read the tiny print below the photograph. *Honfleur,* it said, *Calvados.*

She could not breathe for anguish. *Go back. It doesn't matter what he might have done . . . what he did . . . what he would do . . . whatever happened to them both. Seize the moment, the day—*

"Can I help you, Miss?"

She swallowed to regain her voice. She said thickly, "I want to go to France."

"Yes. Any special part, or just Paris? Paris will be direct."

"Paris will be all right." She would arrange about Honfleur when she got to Paris; she would cover her traces that way, in case anyone wanted to find her.

"Round trip? For how many days?"

"I don't know."

"We have a number of fourteen-day to three-week charter trips I could put you on—"

"Couldn't I have just a one-way ticket to Paris?" She was beginning to panic with his questions.

He looked at her more carefully, and decided that she was odd. "First-class?"

"I . . . suppose so."

"When would you like to leave?"

"At once. Tomorrow."

He looked up. "You have your passport up to date?"

"Passport?" She flushed. "I don't have a passport."

He put down his pencil. "First thing you have to do is get a passport," he said. "You can go to the post office on Cedar and fill out a form. It should take about ten days to three weeks. You can phone me when you get it, and we can make travel arrangements then."

Disconcerted, she stared at him.

"Three weeks should take you just past Christmas. You might want to spend Christmas at home, anyway," he said consolingly. "Tell you what—I'll make a reservation for you about the first week after New Year's. You call me when you get the passport, and I'll send the ticket on to you. Name and address please?"

Again she was disconcerted. "Send the ticket to . . . Mr. William Tieman. He's the lawyer on this street."

"Oh, yes. Mr. Tieman. I know him. I'll just deliver it to him when I hear from you."

Uncle Bill would have to know, then. She must make him promise utter secrecy.

She went down to Cedar Street and filed an application for her passport. It meant further delay, getting a copy of her birth certificate, too, but fortunately the City Hall was on the same street and they were able to print a copy for her while she waited. Even so, it was almost five before she ran back to Uncle Bill's office and caught him as he was about to leave.

"Sit down, Iris," he said, taking off his coat again. "What's the problem?" He knew she never came to him unless there was a problem; otherwise, concerning routine legal matters, he sent for her.

"There is no problem," she said steadily. "I want to travel. I'm going away."

He lifted his eyebrows. "Alone?"

She said, "Is there any reason why I shouldn't go alone?"

His eyebrows remained raised. "None at all," he said briskly. "I'm very glad, Iris, that you are ready to make a move on your own. It's high time. But what about Ralph?"

She looked at him for a few moments without replying, trying to decide how much she could tell him, how much she had to tell him.

"Ralph doesn't know my plans. I don't want him to know that I'm going. I don't want anybody to know *where* I'm going. I want my plans kept a complete secret from everybody."

He sighed, and looked away.

She knew what the sigh meant; it meant, I thought Iris had grown up and was thinking maturely, but instead she is being emotional again and running away from something. Sure enough he said, "You and Ralph have a spat?"

"We haven't had a spat," she said quietly. "I want to go away. My reasons are my own. If you don't think you can handle this, please tell me now, and I will make other arrangements."

This time she had shocked him. "Well!" he said. And again, "Well, Iris, I hardly think that will be necessary. If you want to go off on some secret escapade, I'm sure I will be able to cover up for you."

"It isn't a secret escapade."

"No, of course not. That was merely a manner of speaking."

For a moment she allowed herself a little triumph. It was the first time she had ever rattled Bill Tieman. She had a brief sense of power, and the realization that instead of her coming to him as a frightened suppliant, as she always had, it was she who had made him uneasy. Managing her affairs was probably the most important account he had ever had, or would ever have.

She said, "Remember, I want nobody to know where I am, or why I decided to go. If anyone were to find out, I would consider it an unforgivable breach of confidence."

"I understand, Iris." His manner had subtly changed. He addressed her as a woman. "Could you tell me if there is any reason for you to leave so suddenly? I can be of help, if there is."

She shook her head. "I don't like the house now. It's very large and empty. Aunt Gladys's death was a shock. I need to get away."

208

"I can understand that, but ... so suddenly. And Ralph?"

"I'm not married to Ralph yet," she said. "I may not marry him. I want to think about it a little longer. This is also in strict confidence, Uncle Bill."

He seemed to hesitate. "It would be lying to say I hadn't suspected that you and Dr. Sexton—"

"Dr. Sexton means nothing to me. He's only a friend, and my teacher. He has nothing to do with my leaving, and above all, I want the same secrecy applied to him. If he should inquire, you know nothing."

"The servants—"

"No one must know. My passport and ticket are going to be delivered to your office. Please call me as soon as the passport comes, so I can arrange the departure date, and then I'll drive down here and pick them up."

"Yes, if you want it like that. The house—"

"Have Evans send all bills directly to you. If Dr. Sexton needs anything for the gatehouse, take care of it immediately. He'll probably stay on until June. After that I'll let you know."

He stared. "Does that mean you plan to stay away until June?"

"Maybe longer," she said. "I may even decide to live abroad for a while. I'll be in touch with you when I need money, and I'll tell you where to send it."

"Iris, something is very much the matter, and I wish you would tell me what it is. You just don't pick yourself up this suddenly and take off for an indefinite time—"

"My mother did," she said. "Did you question my mother?"

"Your mother went with your father, which is quite a different matter. You're all alone, you haven't been well—"

"I'm quite well now. And perfectly capable of taking care of myself. This is what I want, and if you can't help me, tell me now."

"I'll do whatever I can. I told you that. But I am concerned."

"It's the way I want things to be."

"Then that's the way it will be."

But she didn't feel as strong as she had pretended to be with Bill Tieman. When she drove back it was dark, and her headlights briefly illuminated the gatehouse as she waited for the gates to open. Sexton was at the window, staring out. He recognized her car, and she saw him start, as if he meant to call out to her, but she put her foot hard on the gas pedal and shot on toward the house, her chest so constricted she could hardly breathe.

Ralph came home on Christmas Eve. Together they trimmed the tree, which they had always done with Aunt Gladys. Gifts had been delivered and placed around it, but the custom was to wait until morning to open them, and she waited, although this Christmas there would only be she and Ralph, and the servants. Even Coffey would not be there; she had taken to her bed the last week. Dr. Nichols said there was nothing specifically wrong, except the deterioration that had been heralded by the stroke, and suddenly now accelerated.

"This is for you, Iris. Someone thinks you need a bottle of Scotch." Ralph gave the rectangular box a shake.

She took it, but almost at once put it aside. It was from Sexton; she recognized his handwriting on the card addressed to her. She managed to bring the box to her room without opening it, and only there did she rip open the envelope.

The note said only, *This has turned mysteriously flat.*

In the box was a half-finished bottle of Calvados.

For a moment she allowed herself to touch the brown pottery bottle with the Norman peasant's head forming the cap, and then she put the bottle in the back of her closet where she would not have to see it again.

They skied on the open slopes of her estate. She wondered if Sexton saw them. She wondered if he was in the gatehouse. Whenever she stepped outside on her balcony to look, the house had only the same small light burning in the front hall. Apparently he never put it out, because she looked during the small hours of the morning when she could not sleep, and it was always burning. Maybe he went away for the holidays and left it on. Twice out of boredom she and Ralph drove into the country to have dinner, but the evenings were curiously silent.

*211*

"How are you getting on with your investigations?"

He shook his head. "Some of them require me to go to New York, and I haven't had the time. I will, though, first chance I get."

"Ralph, why not forget what happened? Why not accept that it was an accident? The police think it was an accident. You're not helping yourself to get over it."

"I'm not interested in forgetting. If anybody hurt my mother, I want to make sure he gets what's coming to him."

It couldn't be for love of Aunt Gladys; it had to be for some other reason. He went on, as if he had read her mind.

"How's your friend Sexton?"

"I don't know," she said. "I stopped the lessons when Aunt Gladys died. He may have gone away while the college is closed. I don't see him anymore."

Perhaps she could put him off that way, but the expression on his face revealed he was unconvinced. He would have to believe her when she went away, and left Ian behind.

Bill Tieman telephoned her the day Ralph left for Boston.

"I didn't call before, though I've had what you're waiting for on my desk since Saturday. I wanted to be sure we wouldn't be overheard, and have it all come out."

212

He was being heavily, magisterially conspiratorial. If her heart hadn't begun to pound at his news, she might have laughed. Actually, there was no need for him to speak so guardedly. There was no one now to listen in on her telephone calls.

She got in touch with the travel agent. He could put her on a plane to Paris by Thursday. He would arrange a flight to New York that would eliminate the need to spend a night in the city; there would be only a few hours' wait at Kennedy. Her tickets would be at Mr. Tieman's office in the morning.

She went upstairs, found a large suitcase and began to pack.

Sexton was back. There were lights in his house that night, and when she drove to Concord to get her tickets, she saw the fresh marks of his tires in the snow beside the gatehouse. When she returned that evening, Evans handed her a note from him. It said only: "Why? Can we talk about it? I'll stop by this evening."

She told Evans that she was not at home to anyone, for any reason.

She didn't say good-bye to Coffey until the morning. Dressed, having told Evans that she was going on a trip and would let him know when she would return, her bag already stowed in the big car, she went upstairs to Coffey's room.

Coffey looked at her in bewilderment. "Why are you going away, Iris?"

"I want to go away, Coffey. I have to. I can't bear it here anymore."

"It's that man Sexton. Doesn't he love you? Is that why he doesn't come here anymore?"

"It has nothing to do with him. I never really cared for him that much. It was just friendship."

"You don't fool me, Iris. You were in love with that man."

"Coffey," she said sternly, "I never loved him, and he never loved me. Do you understand? We were only friends. He was my teacher, and I let him stay in the gatehouse. That's all you know. He was just a friend, you hear?"

She caught the old woman's hands in her intensity. Coffey looked frightened, and began to whimper. Iris put her arms around her and held her and kissed her. "Everything's all right, Coffey. Just remember, Dr. Sexton is nothing to me and never was."

"You're angry at me," Coffey whimpered. "You know I despised that woman, that aunt of yours, and now that she's dead you hate me for it, and you're going away and leaving me."

"No, Coffey. My going away has nothing to do with that. I just . . . need to get away. That's all. I'll write you."

She escaped.

She got into the car with Wolfe and they went down the drive. At the gates she stopped. "Will you drop this in the mail slot of Dr. Sexton's door?" she said to Wolfe. "It's a report I did for class, and I want to make sure I get credit for it."

It seemed like a sensible smoke screen, to follow through on the motions of their relationship, teacher

214

and pupil, and so she had hurriedly written a paper on the Cavalier poets. On the first page she had written Ian a brief note. She watched Wolfe drop the envelope in the gatehouse slot and felt a terrible sense of finality. Better this way, better to end it now before there is any further tragedy. They went on toward the airport.

# 15

*H*e drove down to New York for Christmas. He knew Ralph would be there at the Castle with Iris, and he felt she would be less uneasy if he were not around. He didn't believe the break between him and Iris was final. He thought she was very disturbed over her aunt's death, but that would pass. Even if she guessed about Sally, he did not think it would be enough to turn her away from him completely, and besides, she could not be sure. Sally had not had time to tell her, unless she had written a note at once, and he sensed that Sally would have preferred to save the tidbit for a time when she could be face to face with Iris and enjoy the reaction. The aunt might have worked Iris over, but he didn't think Iris would have swallowed whole anything the aunt told her at that point.

Getting away from Freebody would be good for him. He needed a chance to clear his mind of the whole atmosphere. He couldn't escape talk of the two deaths; because he lived on the estate, everyone thought he had access to special information. Even when he turned up at Dodie's and Jeff's, it was a signal to bring up the topic of Sally and Mrs. Forsher. Someone even said jokingly that he was surprised that Iris hadn't done away with the two of them herself. "Sally Lucas had her teeth in Iris ever since the boy hanged himself. I hear she sent her anonymous notes from time to time, rubbing it in. And the aunt had her under her thumb so the girl couldn't do a thing on her own."

His sense of humor seemed to have deserted him. "I don't see Iris Freebody trailing Sally on some dark night and holding her head underwater. She isn't the type. And the aunt's death was an accident. Everyone accepts that."

"Ian, you're taking it so personally."

He raised his voice, "Don't you have anything better to do than cut the girl to ribbons?"

"Ian, I'm beginning to think you like her," said Dodie.

"Yes, I like her. She's a gentle, shy girl who never did anybody any harm. She was damned generous about the gatehouse. Why should I dislike her?"

"Don't get so excited, Ian," Dodie said. "It's only because we're marooned up here in this land of ice and snow when we'd rather be basking in the sun somewhere, and we have to warm ourselves with gossip. No one is serious."

So he went down to New York for the balance of the holiday. He checked into a hotel, saw friends, went to the theater. He even drove to Brooklyn, parked in front of the old house and walked around it. It was sold now, and he couldn't go in if he wanted to, but the important thing was that he could bear to look at it at all. Maybe if he had been able to go in, he would have exorcised Frannie completely, but even as it was, he thought he was making a fine recovery. Unless it was just that his mind had no room for anything now but trying to understand Iris's behavior.

He drove back to Freebody on New Year's Day, knowing that Ralph would be going back to Cambridge that day for classes the next morning. The first thing he did was leave a note for Iris with Evans. Iris was out, Evans told him, and so he asked in his note if he could see her later that evening. He was sure she wasn't out the first time, and when he came back later Evans conveyed Iris's message that she could not see him.

If that's the way she wants it, that's the way it will be, he said to himself. He went back to the gatehouse, resolved that even if she came to his door he would be cool, as if there had never been anything between them—not their kiss, not her confession that she wanted him on any terms.

It was several evenings later that he came home and found a brown manila envelope pushed through the mail slot. He was painfully affected by the sight of her handwriting; he carried the envelope to the living room to open it.

A sheaf of typed pages fell out, titled: *The Wit of the Cavalier Poets*. His mouth fell open in disbelief. A single piece of notepaper lay on top, handwritten. It said:

Dear Ian,
When you receive this, I will be gone. Please don't look for me, or ask anybody where I am. Nobody knows anyway. I don't want people to think that where I am is of any concern to you, if it is, and I hope it isn't, by now. As you said, it was the sort of thing a patient feels for her psychiatrist, and it's over, and I'm well again. Please stay on in the gatehouse for the balance of the year. It's yours, and I will not be back before that. Thank you for the great help you've been to me.

Iris

His first reaction was a gust of helpless rage. He crumpled the note and tossed it across the room, where it lay on the hearth looking as defenseless and vulnerable as Iris herself. He suddenly felt as if he had abused her as well as the note, and he got up to retrieve it, and smoothed it carefully on his knee.

He said to himself, Well, man, that's that. And now forget her. You didn't even know you wanted her; you almost convinced yourself you didn't. You had her in the palm of your hand for a while, and you gave yourself up to speculation as to whether you were ready to accept such a gift of wholehearted, unrestrained love, plus the millions that went with it. You've been trying to convince yourself that it doesn't matter. Only it does matter.

Maybe it's just my bruised ego, he told himself. Maybe he had been too cocky, because she seemed so anxious, because she defied her aunt and her fiancé, gave him the house, put off the wedding, told him it didn't even matter if he were a fortune hunter, opened her lips for his kiss as if he had the gift of life to place between them like a sacrament. Maybe now it hurt because she had withdrawn it all so summarily, without a word of explanation that he could believe.

He didn't believe she was better and thank you for your help. There was something else, there had to be. Damn her, she was a fool, almost as great a fool as he. Together he could have shown her how to live and love; she would have learned what she was and what she had to give, and how she held the world in her two hands and didn't know it. To walk out like that, without giving him a chance to reason with her, to explain himself, to make amends if any were necessary.

He put on his coat and trudged bleakly through the snow to the castle and rang the bell. Evans opened the door.

"So she's gone," Ian said. "Do you know where she went? Or why?"

"She never told any of us her plans," Evans said. "The first I knew of it, she asked me to tell Wolfe to bring the car around to take her to the airport. Miss Freebody always was a strange little girl, always sort of frightened, and by herself. There's no telling what she'll do, and I don't mind saying we are all worried about her."

"She must have told someone. She must have made some arrangements. She couldn't have walked out on a household like this without some preparations."

"Mr. Tieman phoned this afternoon," Evans said.

"Everything is to go on as usual here, until she comes back. He will run the estate for her."

"Mr. Tieman. That's the lawyer. Where does he live?"

"I only have the address of his law offices in Concord. He's a very private man, which is why the Freebody family trusted him. I'm sure Miss Freebody knows where his home is, but of course I wouldn't know that."

Too late to see him in his office. He thought. "Didn't she speak to Coffey?"

"Yes, she did. I don't know what she told her. Miss Coffey stays in her bed now. She's failing, we think."

"Could I go up to see her?"

"Let me ask her first."

The house had the hushed, lifeless quality that the gatehouse now possessed. Odd, for a quiet girl she seemed to have lent animation and warmth that no one had even been aware of, as if both houses responded to her presence. He felt abandoned. That was it. She had abandoned them.

"You can go up to see her, Dr. Sexton. But don't stay too long, please, because she gets very tired and starts to cry."

"Right," Ian said, and went up the stairs.

As soon as she saw him, she said, "What happened between you? I was sure it was going to be all right. I wanted so much for her to be happy. I would have done anything to make her happy. Anything!"

"I know," he said. "But, Coffey, maybe we were both wrong and maybe we assumed too much. We

*221*

thought we knew her, but apparently we didn't."

"I know her," she said. "She never had any real mother but me, and I knew what she felt by the look on her face. She could never hide anything from me. Dr. Sexton, she's in love with you, and now I'm frightened for what she may do. Or what someone may do to her. You've got to find her and bring her back."

"Help me then," he said "Where did she go?"

"I think she went to Europe," she said. "It's where her mother would run off to at the drop of a hat, and Iris would think of Europe if she had to run anywhere."

"But didn't she give you even a hint as to where she might be heading?"

She shook her head. "She was angry at me. She knew I couldn't stand that creature that called herself her aunt. Harpy that she was, she wanted Iris dead. She would have killed her, too, somehow, I know. And now Iris blames me. She won't stay in the same house with me. Maybe she ran away because of me."

Her voice trailed off. The tears in the corners of her eyes seemed to lack the energy to roll down, and stayed there.

"Miss Coffey, Iris's aunt died accidentally. It happens all the time, and there's no reason to blame anyone, and Iris knows that. I'm going to see Mr. Tieman tomorrow, and maybe he can help me. I'll keep in touch."

She struggled to sit up. He helped her and put the pillows behind her back.

"Dr. Sexton, please, in the top drawer in the bureau

222

is a box of stationery. Would you hand it to me, please?"

He opened the drawer in which her possessions lay piled neatly, handkerchiefs, stockings, a box of face powder, a flowered box of writing paper with a pen in a loop on top of it, all wreathed in an old-lady smell of violets. He handed the box to her.

"I have to write Iris a letter," she said.

"But where will you send it?"

"I'll send it to Mr. Tieman. He'll know how to get it to her."

Tieman must know where she was.

He had to wait until his last class was over, but fortunately this was his short day and he got to Concord late in the afternoon. A secretary had him sit on a bench in the outer office until a buzzer sounded, and then the secretary ushered out a thin old man leaning on a cane. Old old old. Everyone connected with Iris seemed to be old. No wonder Ralph must have descended on her life like a god. Or even he, for that matter, though he was in his thirties and over the hill to the young. But young in Iris's frame of reference. She could be a prey to the first young opportunist who learned she had money. He could see her turning to some stranger in gratitude for his companionship, not troubling to know who he was any more than she cared to learn the background of the man she had invited to live on her estate—about Frannie, about . . . anything. Damn her, she could be married before he found her.

"Mr. Tieman will see you now."

The man behind the desk was short and stout and ruddy and bald. The fringe of hair over his ears was white. Old old old.

"Dr. Sexton. Sit down, please."

Ian sat down. He said, "Iris wrote me a note telling me she was going away for an indefinite time and not to look for her. I have to find her."

"I'd like to help you, but I can't. It's my professional obligation to respect a client's secrecy, and she asked me to be secret. Just as she told you not to look for her. I think she's made her intentions very plain."

They sat staring at each other for a moment. "Look," Ian said, "certain phrases in her letter suggest that she is doing this because . . . well, that I . . . I may have something to do with her leaving. If that's so, this may be all for nothing, and there might be no reason for her to disappear."

"What phrases, for instance?"

"Well, things like, she doesn't want people to think I am concerned about her. I have a feeling that she wishes to make it clear to everybody that we were not . . . involved with each other."

"Were you?"

He didn't answer at once.

Tieman said, "I asked her something like that. She denied it vigorously."

"But she would have to, wouldn't she, if she felt it had to be denied, if that's why she ran away."

"You're rather arrogant, Dr. Sexton, if I may say so. Aren't you taking a great deal for granted? Your importance in Miss Freebody's life, for instance? After all, she is engaged to marry Ralph Forsher. Though ..." Tieman hesitated "... she did somehow suggest that she was not certain in her own mind about him."

Ian let out his breath in a grunt of relief. "I'm glad about that much. I was afraid she might marry him so that he wouldn't be deprived of her money, as well as a home, with Mrs. Forsher dead."

Tieman looked at him sharply. "And speaking of Miss Freebody's estate," he said, his glance level under two brushes of white eyebrows, "I imagine you are aware of the terms of her will?"

"Iris mentioned it to me, and so did Coffey."

"Then you know that her husband will be the sole heir to her estate if she should die in the married state. Miss Freebody's mother had this kind of will drawn up to exclude members of her own family from the benefit of her money, and Iris wanted the same arrangement."

"I gathered that," he said steadily. "I am also aware that if Miss Freebody were to die before she was married, her money would go entirely to Ralph Forsher."

"What are you suggesting?"

"No more than you were."

"Look here," Tieman said, "I have no reason to believe that your regard for Miss Freebody is any more or less sincere than Mr. Forsher's. I am sure you both find Miss Freebody a very attractive person and want to marry her for that reason. This whole conversation is pointless, in a way, since I do not know where Miss Freebody is, and if I did, I gave her my word I would keep it a secret."

"Even if you thought she was in danger?" Ian cried.

Tieman looked disconcerted, briefly. "I don't believe she is in any danger," he said slowly. "Why should she be in any danger?"

"Even from herself! She's never been away alone. She's in a strange place, wherever it is, and friendless, and her frame of mind can't be too happy, considering her aunt's death, which seemed to shock her very much. There's no telling what she may do!"

Tieman stared at him a long time. He seemed shaken, and for a moment Ian's hope leaped—he's going to tell me. But then Tieman said, "I don't know where she is. She is going to keep in touch with me, she says, but unless I hear from her, I have no idea of her whereabouts. I have to wait for some communication from her. That was the way she wanted it, and I could not change her mind." He hesitated. "If circumstances change, and I should know from her letter, when I get it, I may be able to tell you more."

He had to believe that Tieman was telling the truth. And yet . . . something . . . He was holding back something.

Still deep in thought, Ian left the office and walked to his car. A flashing neon light caught his eye: Concord Travel. It stopped him dead. She had to get her ticket somewhere. There was no place in Freebody. Where else did she ever go but Concord, and where else but to Tieman's office? It was just a hunch, of course, but worth a try.

He entered the office of Concord Travel. A young man behind the counter looked up.

"Yes? Can I help you?"

"I'm thinking about a trip to Europe. I've just come from Mr. Tieman's office—you know Tieman, the lawyer down the street?" An instant flash of recognition came over the man's face; it might or might not be encouraging. "He told me you arranged something for a young woman who's a client of his—"

The young man didn't even let him finish. "Sure, I remember her. I sold her a first-class ticket to Paris. One-way, which we don't often sell up here. Made her stick in my mind. I don't think she even knew where she was going when she walked in. She seemed to decide as she went along."

"Yes, well . . ." He was elated. That had to be Iris. So now he knew she was in Paris, anyway, or in France at least. "I just wanted to get an idea about what the fare will run. I haven't made up my mind yet when I'm leaving."

He spent a little more time, to cover the fact that he had already found what he came for, and started out with folders and a notation about what it would cost to fly to Paris and return. Almost as an afterthought, he asked casually, "Did she mention any other places she might be going to? I might look her up when I get there."

He drew a blank. The man shook his head. "Like I said, I don't think she knew herself. Studied the posters, though."

She was in France. How the devil do you find someone in France who doesn't want to be found? And how could he go there? He couldn't just walk out on his job, not if he expected ever to be hired by any decent university again. He had to give them time to get someone to take over his classes. Freebody had no intersession, only a long spring vacation that began the middle of February and went on into Easter. Maybe they could get someone to fill his job just until spring vacation began.

But even that lapse of time was too much. Anything could happen in six weeks if she were desperate enough, and she must have been desperate to summon the determination to take off on her own. And what would Forsher do? Wouldn't Forsher take after her as soon as he could, and wouldn't she fall into his arms if he appeared? But how could Forsher find her any more than he could?

And what would happen to her in the meantime?

# 16

*T*he plane landed at Orly in the morning. She took her bag and cleared Customs and came out into the crowded terminal. Ahead was a desk with a sign over it which said in English: Welcome to France. And below it: Information. She dragged her bag over with her and stood in line until a uniformed girl turned to her.

"Yes? May I help you?"

"I would like to go to Honfleur."

The girl looked at her as if she were mad. "At this time of year, Madame? Most of the tourist hotels will be closed—unless you are visiting friends?"

"Yes. I'm visiting friends."

"Do you know Paris at all?"

"No."

"Then perhaps it would be best to hire a taxi to take you to American Express or Cooks, where they will have train and bus schedules. Just tell the driver to take you to one of those places."

She went outside. Behind the yellow buses drawn up

to the sidewalk were taxis. A driver jumped out to put her bag in the trunk. "The American Express office," she said. "In Paris." He opened the door for her.

At least this much was simple.

They drove over a crowded autoroute into the mesh of traffic that was Paris. She saw the Eiffel Tower quite close, but yet curiously far away, as if she were seeing it on film as a travelogue. They were crossing the Seine, and now she caught a brief glimpse of the Opera before the taxi stopped just beyond it, and she was deposited with her baggage on the step of the American Express office. She held out to the driver the francs she had bought at Kennedy, and he selected what he wanted.

So—she had come a little farther and it was still simple.

Inside there were Americans, and American voices behind the desks. "I want to go to Honfleur." She followed the pointing finger. Schedules were consulted. There was a train from Saint Lazare leaving within the hour. Yes, she could make it easily; it was moments away by taxi. The train would take her to Caen, where she could find a bus to Honfleur.

"Excuse me," said the girl behind the desk, "but why would you want to go to Honfleur at this time of year?"

"I'm visiting friends," she said.

Taxi, train. She had a sense of triumph as she settled herself against the green plush seat of her compartment and watched the countryside replace Paris—brown fields, gunmetal spirals of river, leafless trees, low stone villages with slate roofs. She had lunch at the Caen station, waiting for the bus. It left half empty; it was cold, and rattled.

Along the route snow began to fall, plastering itself against the windows. In the towns they went through, people bent their heads against the cold. She shivered. The road grew smaller, the landscape more like a picture postcard. The familiar gnarled shapes of the apple trees were iced in white; there was thatch on the roofs, and the houses were low and half-timbered, as Sexton had described. Sexton. She swallowed and knew she did not dare let herself think about him.

The bus rattled down a cobbled street and left her midway. She took her bag and continued on foot. The streets were narrow, widening only at the bottom when she reached the harbor. It was rimmed by leaning ancient houses. Boats creaked on their ropes moored to the stone breakwater. It was beautiful, as Sexton had said. And no motels. In fact, there was no one in sight.

A large russet dog guarded the door of a café. She stepped past him and went inside. She had to duck her head, the ceiling was so low. A man was drying glasses behind a tiny bar.

"Do you know where I can rent a room?"

He smiled at her, uncomprehending.

She remembered her French from Miss Ames. At Miss Ames they concentrated on French. "Je voudrais . . . louer une chambre."

"Ah!"

But then he frowned, and shook his head. Her heart

sank. She did not want to go back to Caen, which was a large town and not particularly pretty on first view. Honfleur was small; it suited her. Besides, she felt at home here; Ian knew Honfleur.

Now he was nodding slowly, still frowning, telling her there was a pension. Perhaps they were open—he did not know. Mme. Bezard and her husband went away in the winter . . . they had a daughter living in the South. . . . He came to the door with her, and pointed out the direction. She followed, past the harbor, past the small deserted square, up the hill again. The wind blew savagely at her back, and her shoes were sodden. There was a wooden gate on her right, as the man had described, too tall to see over, set in thick hedges. A white gull was painted on the gate, and above it, was lettered: La Mouette. She pulled at a rusted iron bell.

After some minutes she was ready to turn away—in all probability the Bezards had gone south—when half the gate opened inward a little and an old man looked out.

"Oui?"

She said in French, "You have rooms to rent?"

He hesitated, and then opened the gate wide enough for her to come in. "You must speak to Madame Bezard."

They went through a garden where a row of leafless, topless trees lined the gravel walk, and where the shrubs beyond were pinched and mournful, as if summer were inconceivable. The door was ajar; she was ushered into a narrow hall half taken up with a stairway. A woman came toward them, stout, in a dark

232

dress, her enormous bosom a shelf on which lay crumbs from luncheon. The man spoke to her, his words and her reply uttered in French too rapid for Iris to follow. The woman's glance rested on her sharply. She thought of Aunt Glad, appraising, judging, too sharply to be kind.

"We are not open at this season, " Mme. Bezard said. "You would have to take your meals at the café, except for the petit dejeuner which I would bring to your room."

Iris let out her breath in relief. "That would be fine."

They went up the narrow stairs, M. Bezard carrying her bag. A door was opened, and a small room loomed beyond, dominated by a wide bed under a flowered quilt. The sloped ceiling was covered in flowered paper. Iris went to the long windows and pushed one open. Below lay the sea, at the end of a sandy shore; beyond, far away across an estuary, flames flared out of smokestacks.

"Le Havre," said Mme. Bezard. "The chimneys of Le Havre."

"It's very nice," Iris said. "I will take it."

"That will be eighty francs," said Mme. Bezard. "With the petit dejeuner."

Eighty francs. She calculated hastily. About twenty dollars. "A day?" she asked.

Mme. Bezard looked at her keenly. "The week," she said, and added quickly, "plus taxes and service, you understand, yes?"

"Yes."

Mme. Bezard turned the knob on the radiator, which began to clank, emitting the smell of steam. "The bathroom is there. You will have sole use of it at this time, since we have no other guests." She added, tentatively, a little warily, "A bath will cost five francs."

Yes to that, too.

She was left alone. She opened her bag on the luggage rack and hung the few clothes she had brought in the armoire. She put her damp shoes near the radiator to dry, and put out her travel clock and the magazines she had bought at Kennedy. The room was beginning to be pleasantly stuffy. She lay down on the bed and stared toward the chimneys of Le Havre.

From now on, it would be less simple.

# 17

They couldn't get anyone to take over his classes, and he could not walk out on them. It wouldn't be fair to Jeff, who had recommended him. And besides, if he found her, which was unlikely, there was a good chance she would have nothing to do with him, and he would need a job to come home to. But he was restless and uneasy all the time; he checked with the house constantly, and with Tieman, but there was no word from her, or if there was, they weren't giving it out.

At last, just about a week before the holiday would have begun anyway, they found a substitute for him—a graduate student who had come back inquiring about a job in September. The last class over, Ian went to the office and began clearing his desk. Garson was there, one of the assistant professors.

"What's your hurry to go to Europe at this time of year, Sexton? Want to get in some spring skiing?"

"Among other things." It was as good a reason as any to spread around. He didn't want any connection made between his trip and the brief notice in the newspaper that Miss Iris Freebody was on an extended vacation, traveling. It was enough that people asked him where she'd gone, as if living on the estate made him privy to what went on there. "I wouldn't mind a good rest, too. It's been a tough year for me."

Garson said, "If it's a rest you want, *and* skiing, I can recommend a spot called Arosa. It's about the highest of all the resorts in Switzerland and the snow stays a long time, but for some damned reason, the season ends around this time. You'd have the slopes to yourself, as well as any hotel you'd still find open."

"Thanks. I might just go there. How did you find it?" He kept up the show of interest as he piled things in the closet, knowing it was a good way to throw Garson or anybody off his track.

"Actually, my wife's family has a chalet there. They only go up for a month or so, and then the rest of the year a caretaker lives in it. Say," Garson said slowly, "would *you* like to stay in it? I'm sure it could be arranged, if you want it."

"Thanks. That would be great. If I want it, I could wire you, couldn't I?"

"Sure. It's the Oehrli place, if you turn up unexpectedly. Tell them you're a member of the family, from America, and they'll welcome you." Garson even took the trouble to spell the name.

He told Garson again that it was a great idea, and he appreciated it, and managed to get out and drive to Concord in time to get his plane ticket. The travel agent there deserved a break from him after tipping

236

him off about where Iris was. While he was waiting for the ticket to be written up, he wandered around looking at the posters. The clerk's words came back to him from that previous visit here. Studied the posters, he'd said. Iris had studied the posters. He looked at them more carefully. Suddenly his heart bounded. Honfleur. She must have seen the poster of Honfleur.

Somehow he knew she would have gone to Honfleur.

He left with his ticket and a new sense of certainty that he was going to find her. Of course she could have gone, and seen the place, and gone away again by now. There was nothing much to keep her on that cold windy coast in March. He wouldn't allow himself to think about it. He was shaking in his eagerness to be on his way.

At the gatehouse he put some things in a suitcase, covered the hood of his car with an old blanket, checked once more with Evans—nothing—and with Tieman—nothing—and then asked Jeff to drive him to the airport.

He arrived in Paris and allowed himself a minimum time to check the hotels and American Express and Cooks, to see if anybody knew the name and address of Iris Freebody. Finding anyone in Europe, unless the person was in trouble with the police, was a job for a professional. He wasted no more time, rented a car and drove directly to Honfleur. He did not allow himself to think what he would do if she wasn't there.

Honfleur hadn't changed at all. Maybe it was different in the summer when the tourists came, but now

237

the rain-drenched streets were the way he remembered them. Where the devil could she have found a place to stay here?

He drove up and down the streets until he found a small, pleasant hotel that had just reopened. The owners knew nothing about an American girl; there was only one other guest, a commercial traveler, French, but then the hotel had only been open since the fifteenth of February. He decided he might as well stay here.

They gave him a neat room, and he unpacked. There was no point in searching the town tonight; it was raining too hard for anyone to leave a warm house voluntarily. If the weather had been like this up to now—and he presumed it had—she wouldn't have stayed. Why should she? She would have seen it, satisfied herself, and then, more confident by now, moved on to more clement places, maybe even back to Paris.

He went down to the small, cozy bar, where there was a fire, and ordered a drink. In a short while a large man with a ruddy face joined him, nodded, and ordered some cider.

"Americain?"

Ian said yes.

In halting English the man said, "Why does an American come to Honfleur at this season?" He laughed heartily, and touched his head. "Or are you an artist? Or a poet?"

The barman was listening. He said something in French to the man, and the man said, "Our host here says there is another American here, so perhaps it is becoming chic, yes?"

Ian tried to sound only remotely interested. "An American girl?"

More conversation in French, of which he understood only a few words.

"A young woman. She eats at the café near the harbor every day."

"She does? What's the name of the café?"

"La Petite Navire. Near the clock tower."

Ian got up at once, to the vast amusement of the large man. "Lonely, eh?"

He found the café easily and went in, taking a table well away from the window in case she should see him and be frightened off. The waiter came and handed him a handwritten menu. He studied it a moment and then, without raising his eyes, he said casually, "Has the Americaine dined yet?"

"Not yet. Perhaps she won't come in this rain."

He ordered some mussels and a bottle of wine. He would want to stretch the meal out as long as possible. His mouth was so dry that the pieces of bread stuck in his throat, but he did not want to drink the wine yet; he wanted a clear head. She was here. Oh, the Americaine might be another girl, but he was almost sure it was she. She might run away when she saw him. She might refuse to speak to him. The reasons that drove her here must be very powerful, and he would not change her mind that easily. *I must handle her very carefully. I must not frighten her.* He thought of the image that had come to him before, of a bird nestling in the palm of his hand, strangely unafraid, strangely at home there. Only this time it would be different. She had wanted an ocean between them; even more, she had wanted to vanish completely. He would have to win her confidence slowly and carefully, to make her talk, to explain herself.

The door opened and a gust of wet wind blew in with the tall girl who entered in a glistening yellow slicker, her hair plastered to her head.

Iris.

Like someone completely familiar here, she stopped at the door to hang up her dripping raincoat, calling out, "Bon soir," as she turned around. She saw him, and for an instant he thought she would faint. He got to his feet hurriedly, but she was already running the few feet that separated them.

"Ian. Ian."

She was in his arms, clutching him so tightly that his arms hurt afterward where her fingers dug in, and he wondered how he could ever have doubted what she would do.

Somehow they managed to get through the meal, mainly because the waiter observed them keenly and seemed to understand that what was transpiring was a moment of great emotional importance to them which rendered them oblivious to everything else. Or so they explained it to themselves afterward, laughing. At any rate, the waiter quickly put down two dishes of hot food, which they ate, and wine, which they drank, and then the coffee.

*240*

It had stopped raining by the time they left the café, and a few bluish stars glittered behind shifting clouds. He forgot about the car as they walked toward her pension. She still hadn't told him why she had run away. In fact, she hadn't even mentioned Freebody. They spoke only of her trip here, and living in Honfleur, and how she walked mainly—or went to the ciné when there was one—and why she had chosen Honfleur; and he told her why he had not come sooner, and why he had known somehow that she would be here.

Only in the tiny velvet and marble parlor of Mme. Bezard's house did he get around to asking her. "But *why*, Iris?"

Up to now her face had seemed almost translucent, so lit from within. But now the light was extinguished, and he thought of how she had looked after her aunt died. It took her moments before she framed an answer.

"I couldn't bear it there, after . . . what happened. They couldn't get rid of the smell of smoke, no matter what they did—paint, spray, everything."

It wasn't the whole truth, he knew. "Why did you have to run? Couldn't you have explained how you felt—everyone would have understood—and just gone off like a reasonable person, leaving some kind of for-warding address?"

This time she took even longer to answer, and her voice grew even more colorless. "I don't want to talk about it, Ian."

"You should. Get it out of your system."

She turned her head away. "I'm a jinx, that's all. I . . . seem to create unhappiness."

"You know that's nonsense. You're not being serious, are you?"

"Yes," she said.

They sat in silence. "What was in your mind? To stay away forever?"

"To stay away until . . . you went away."

He studied her. "Was it me you were afraid to jinx?"

"Yes."

"And you left so as not to jinx me?"

"Yes."

"Idiot," he said, relief rushing up into his throat so he could hardly get the words out. "You know what? I'm going to marry you right away and prove to you how wrong you are."

She didn't answer.

He said, "Will you? Do you want to?"

She was crying. "I want to. But I'm . . . afraid."

"I'll be with you," he said. "There'll be nothing to be afraid of from now on."

She was shaking her head, and wiping her eyes with the back of her hand. "I want to. But I can't."

"It's the money, isn't it? That's the jinx, right? Look, I'll show you how to enjoy it."

There was still the slow, hopeless shake of her head.

"Are you afraid I'm after your money? You once said you didn't care if I was, it wouldn't make any difference."

"I'm afraid of what will happen to us."

"Nothing will happen to us. Look, Iris," he said,

taking her hands, "give me a chance to show you you're wrong. Let's have a try at it, anyway. Nothing irrevocable. If we've made a mistake, we can undo it."

"Some mistakes can't be undone. Like Robbie. Like Sally. Like Aunt Gladys."

"What have they got to do with us now?" he said roughly, dropping her hands in his anger and getting to his feet. "That's over, they're dead, and we're alive, and young, and capable of pleasure. That's all you should think about."

She was shaken, at least.

"Why do you want to marry me, Ian?"

He was dumbfounded. "Because . . . I want to. I want to spend my time with you. I'm . . . in love with you."

She said, "Are you in love with me the way you were with your wife? Is it in your pores, in your breath?"

He flushed. She had remembered each word of that wild outburst he had made when he was trying to convince her she didn't know what love was, with Ralph.

He said, "I was half out of my mind when you left. Isn't that enough, Iris? To start with? The rest will come."

She lifted her eyes to him. "I feel the way you said you did. It's in every moment, with me."

For a moment he didn't quite take it in, the way he hadn't when she gave him the gatehouse. Then he began to laugh. He seized her and pulled her to her feet and hugged her and kissed her. Color came back to her face, and she laughed at him, and kissed him back. Her landlady came to the open door to see what was going on, and Iris said to her, "I am going to be married, Mme. Bezard."

More outcries. In a few moments Mme. Bezard returned with a little tray on which were a silver decanter and four tiny glasses. They toasted the moment with thimblefuls of strong, sweet liqueur, M. Bezard appearing for his drink and shaking hands with a surprisingly strong grip.

"Where will the wedding be?" asked Mme. Bezard. "And when?"

"Here, if we can," Iris said.

"And right away. Perhaps tomorrow," he said. "I'll go down to your city hall, or whatever you have, in the morning, and see what arrangements we can make."

He left her later and walked back to his hotel, still forgetting about the car parked in the harbor. It didn't matter. Let them give him a ticket; it still didn't matter. Let someone steal it; it still didn't matter. Elation surged within him, boiling over. The world had become infinite, its pleasures inexhaustible.

# *18*

*L*et it all be a mirage, this happiness—it didn't matter; she would just enjoy it while it lasted; she wouldn't allow herself to think of anything else. His coming had changed everything. Her room was beautiful. Honfleur was beautiful. She was beautiful. Even the weather was beautiful, as if he had changed that, too. The sun was bright, the air cold and crisp, the water sparkled blue and white, the ships bobbed gaily, the air smelled of salt and strong coffee and fresh-baked bread.

But almost at once they ran into a snag with their wedding plans. They could not get married in France unless she was a resident, and she had not obtained a visa to stay. It would take a month for that.

Ian got on the telephone and called the embassy in Paris. "It seems to me I've heard of Americans being married in the embassy." But someone at the embassy told him they were not empowered to marry anyone.

She was standing beside him when he phoned, and

she heard him say with exasperation, "But there must be some way we can be married without waiting a month!" And then, "Switzerland? How do we go about that?" He wrote busily for a while, stopping now and then to have a word spelled out. When he hung up he said, "This may take a couple of weeks. We can be married in Switzerland if we get the necessary papers from the embassy in Bern."

He compressed his mouth ruefully. "And to get *those*, we first have to have some documents from home. Like birth certificates, affidavits of citizenship, divorce or death certificates if either of us were married before. That involves me."

"We could wire, and make it sound urgent."

They wired, and made it sound urgent. They had the certificates sent directly to Bern, to save time. He telephoned Bern as well, to make sure they were satisfying every condition. Then they packed, said goodbye to the Bezards and drove to Paris.

As they entered the city he said, "The next few weeks are on me, if you don't mind, so please don't thrust any large bills at me." He smiled to make his words a joke, but she knew he was serious. "We may have to be frugal. Actually, I'm saving my money to buy you a ring."

The division of their money would be a problem. She wished she could tell him to be as extravagant as he wanted, that there was enough deposited in the Morgan Bank in Paris under her name to hold them for a long time, but she did not know how to say it. She couldn't call on Bill Tieman for help, although he would be able to come up with a working arrangement. She didn't want Uncle Bill to know they were going to be married. She didn't want anyone to know. When she said she would marry him, the thought had flashed almost simultaneously across her mind: But no one must know! If it would help keep it a secret longer, she was prepared to live in Europe as long as necessary, for however long it took for people to forget about Sally and Aunt Gladys.

They checked into a pleasant small hotel he knew off the Place Vendôme. It had a glassed-in box for the concierge, and an open courtyard filled with little tables and potted plants, and it looked more like the Paris of her imagination than she had dared hope for after the bristling thrust of skyscrapers they had passed.

He said to her, "I'm not rushing you, understand. I can wait for the go-ahead from Bern if it's what you want. What I'm saying is, shall I ask for two rooms, or one?"

"One."

Loving and being loved was transfiguring. If his coming had changed everything, their lying together and loving each other was even more profound. It did not seem like the same city she had first come to and looked at as if it were on film. She was part of it; it was hers.

They walked the streets and bought her a trousseau. They drove out into the country to lunch, and all the way back she thought of making love. They drank wine and walked along the Seine, imperishably lovely, and hurried back to the hotel to make love. She forgot that Freebody existed—or Sally, or Ralph, or Aunt Gladys—except in flashes, like stabs. She felt they were existing inside a precious and fragile bubble, and that as long as they stayed within it, floating, hidden, they could be happy.

One day the message came from Bern that their papers were ready; they could come and pick them up. He disappeared for a few hours, giving her time to pack her new clothes in her new suitcases, and when he came back he had a present for her. It was a ring made in the form of a cluster of grapes, each grape an opal with a diamond seed, and a branch of enamel and gold.

"It's so beautiful! Ian, you spent too much money."

He put it on her finger, his face inscrutable. "I have a rich wife now. Or will have, in a day or two."

"Ian. You know what I mean." He had even insisted on buying her clothes, and they had been expensive. He saw her very real distress, and smiled.

"I came into some money. Not much, but I can afford to keep you for a while."

They flew to Bern, picked up the necessary papers, and were married the next morning in some civic building by a man with the imposing title of *Zivilstandsbeamter*. The ceremony was perfunctory, the witnesses unknown, the day gray with scattered snow like flocking on the air. He had rented a car, and they checked out of their hotel at once and headed for the mountains. She didn't care where they went. She was drunk with happiness, so that she was both keenly aware and yet remote.

Ian sang as they drove.

"Are you happy, Ian?"

"Happy isn't the word. I'm mad with joy. Don't I look it?"

He made a fierce face at her, and burst out laughing.

"We've got it all, Iris, don't you see? Is there anything else to want?"

*Me? Do you mean me?*

Somewhere along the road he said, "I suppose we should let a few people know. I'll write Jeff and Dodie. And a sister in Spokane. And some cousins in Washington. You'll probably want to tell Coffey. And Bill Tieman, of course. What about Ralph?"

She was silent. It was as if someone had reached out, some alien hand, and touched the glistening walls of the bubble they were sailing in. "Not yet," she said. "No one has to know yet."

He turned his head in surprise. "Do you want to keep it a secret?"

"Would you mind if we did? Just for a while?"

"Of course not. But why, Iris?"

She lied. "I . . . like it this way. It's private. It just belongs to us."

He was too intelligent to believe her. But he didn't press her any further.

They rode until it grew dark. All along they had been skirting the high Alps, but now in the dusk the mountain terrain loomed suddenly ahead of them, a white and glistening wall, terrifyingly unapproachable.

"Where are we going, Ian? Is it someplace special?"

He stopped on the main street of a town called Chur

to consult the map by the dashboard light. "I was hoping we could make Arosa by tonight. It can't be more than fifteen or twenty miles, but the mileage isn't marked on this map. If you're tired, we can stop here for the night."

"I'm not tired. Twenty miles can't be much. Why Arosa?"

"Someone in the English department offered me his family's chalet. I never expected to take him up on it, but as long as we're in Switzerland, why not? We'll save some money. And I'm not as rich as you are."

He grinned when he said it, but it bothered her that he should be so constantly aware of her money. Couldn't he forget it? She could forget everything, loving him. Why couldn't he forget her money?

They started up again, and a policeman at an intersection pointed to the black arrow marked Arosa. They started to climb almost at once, steeply, on a road that had been scraped but on which snow and ice still lay under a scattering of sand. The road was like a ledge carved out of the mountain, like the paths they used to make at the beach on sand castles, just wide enough to roll a ball down on. The road spiraled, first up one side, then another, and with each curve the lights of Chur sank further and further away until they became only tiny pin pricks before they vanished entirely. Now and then there was a stone guard rail where the drops were especially precipitous, but most of the time there was nothing protecting them from the slopes but the snow-laden pines and a thin wood rail. And sometimes there was nothing.

Somewhere along the road there was a cheering cluster of chalets and a garage, and she tugged at his arm. "Why don't we stay here until morning?"

"Here? Where? Not even a *zimmer frei* sign!" They had seen the room-for-rent signs in German along the route, but none here. He consulted the map. "We can't be very far now, Iris. I called the caretaker from Bern, and he's going to have the place ready for us." He looked at her in the dashboard light. "You're not afraid, are you? You've lived all your life in snow country."

"I've never been on a road like this before."

"Shut your eyes. It can't be more than eight miles from here."

They resumed the endless spiraling upward. Snow began to fall, crusting on the windshield so thickly that he had to get out now and then to wipe it off with a brush. He glanced at her, grinning, each time he got back into the car, and pressed her knee with his hand. "Almost there," he said. "Why are you afraid?"

*Why am I afraid?* Even before he asked it, she had posed the same question to herself. "I have a feeling that . . . everything is so far away. That we are . . . leaving everything behind. Ian, suppose there is a blizzard and we can't get down?"

"Suppose there is?" he said. "Wouldn't it be fun, marooned on top of the world? You wanted to be private. Could you be any more private than this?" When she didn't answer, he went on, "If you really are worried, just think that the Swiss have been coming up here for quite a while, in the snow. And there's a train,

*251*

by the way, that makes a regular run from Chur. That's not as important as that we're together, so why should you be afraid?"

*Why should I be afraid?*

He went on even more slowly as the visibility decreased, and he had to get out more often to brush the windshield clear. All she could see was the tunnel of light ploughed by their headlights, and she was almost glad that she could no longer look down. They passed one car, a small van that stopped and pressed itself to the side of the mountain so that they could squeeze by. She held her breath as they skirted the edge. But Ian laughed at her. He was in high spirits.

Ahead, some lights winked sparsely. They rumbled over a wooden bridge; in the ravine below she thought she saw train tracks. At last they found themselves on a level platter of ground, almost as high as the white peaks that encircled them. In the center was a bluish pond, frozen, and a number of buildings, almost all dark.

"The season's practically over here," he said, "but the caretaker said the Valsana would be open, and he'd leave the key at the desk for us. You wait here." He pulled up at a tall hotel with only a scattering of lights in its windows and went up the steps, which someone had cleared of snow.

In a short while he was out, holding up a key to her. "Just another five minutes from here."

He opened his window to be able to watch for landmarks. The air was thin and icy. Again they went upward, past dark chalets hidden in pines, and now there was a wooden shingle dangling in front of them, with a pair of skis painted on it and the name Oehrli

"This is it!"

The driveway had been dug out so they were able to make it to the porch, and a light had been left burning. All she could see was raw yellow wood planks, and a roof which sloped down to the windows. He brought their luggage up to the porch while she waited there. She was conscious of utter stillness, and utter whiteness, broken only by the dark shapes of the firs. *There is nothing to be afraid of. We're together.*

He opened the door and felt for the switch. Light fell from above on the same raw yellow wood—walls, floor, even furnishings, softened by cushions and a few small rugs. Some heat came from registers in the floor, but there was a tremendous fireplace and huge logs piled in it.

"Let's get this started right away," he said, bending to it.

She wandered off. The kitchen was part of the room, concealed by open shelves on which dishes were piled. The bedroom was up an open flight of stairs, a balcony with just enough room for two beds.

"Well?" he called out triumphantly as the fire leaped furiously behind him. "Isn't this great? I told you there was nothing to be afraid of!"

The beds were made up, piled with quilts, and there was canned food on the shelves, and milk and cheese in the refrigerator. Ian lugged their suitcases upstairs and opened them on the bed, but she fell silent, putting their things away.

253

"Look, are you disappointed?" he said. "If you are, we can move on in the morning. It isn't luxurious, not what you're used to. It's just that Garson offered it to me, and it seemed like a good idea . . ."

"It's just fine, Ian. The Bezards' pension wasn't luxurious, either. I guess it's only that I'm tired, and the drive frightened me, in all that snow. There's a canned ham in the refrigerator. Shall I fix something to eat?"

They pulled a table in front of the fire and ate their supper. When she saw his eyes fixed on her from time to time, as if he were trying to fathom how she felt, she felt impelled to say again, "I'm glad we came here. It will be beautiful in the morning."

After they had cleared away their dishes, he went to the door and pushed it open. The snow had stopped, but already their prints on the porch were obliterated, and a layer of white covered their car.

"The caretaker is going to stop in and see if we need anything. There are skis in the shed, and maybe some of the boots will fit us. Otherwise we'll buy what we need. But I want you to be happy, Iris. If you're not, then I don't want to stay here either."

"I am happy," she said. "I'm very happy."

And she *was* happy later, in his arms, under the pile of feather quilts, with the snow piled against the window.

She was happy whenever they made love in the days that followed, because then there was no chance to think, or wonder: why were they here? why was he so ready to accede to her wish to keep their wedding secret? They were so very alone here. No one stopped by, except the caretaker, and they could barely make themselves understood to him. The sun shone only fitfully, and every day it snowed. When they walked into the village they met almost no one; it was as if everyone stayed inside, or had gone away until the summer.

Was he joking when he had told her he had come into some money? Had he borrowed it, on the strength of her money?

Why had he brought her here?

He seemed buoyed up by excitement, tireless; his spirit never flagged, unlike hers. If he thought about Sally, or Aunt Gladys, he never let her guess. Could he be so convincing an actor if he were concealing something? Could he persuade her almost completely that he loved her, that she was beautiful, that he never remembered being so happy?

He rubbed her cheeks with snow, to make them red, he said. He liked to kiss her out of doors, to warm her cold lips, he said. They made love in front of the fire. There was no one to see them. Ernst, the caretaker, came by in the morning, and after he returned with their food they did not see him again. And so the house was completely theirs.

"Isn't this better than having servants around? Do you realize that never again in your life will you have this kind of isolation? Isn't this better than a hotel?"

*Why had he brought her here?* When he took her in

255

his arms was he thinking: This is only for now, for not too long; one day I can stop pretending that she is beautiful and that I've never been as happy.

He didn't talk of going home, so nothing was settled in his mind. Maybe he was waiting for the last of the skiers to leave, for the town to settle into its remote isolation until the summer. Maybe he planned that they would have at least this much time together. Maybe he was even enjoying it enough to make him want to postpone whatever plans he had. Maybe he even loved her a little. She could almost believe it.

And then Ralph telephoned.

# 19

*T*here had been a telephone call the day before Ralph called. It had startled her because she had thought their presence here unknown, and it seemed as if a rip had been made in the fragile walls of their bubble, and a breath of cold from the outside entered. There was no reason for her sense of foreboding. Ian answered, and his expression grew pleased as he talked, so she knew it couldn't be anything bad.

He was jotting something down on a pad. When he replaced the phone the pleased expression had become elation. "You'll never guess what that was about," he said. "You remember my telling you about the book I've been working on? On medieval narrative? Well, a textbook publisher seems to be interested!"

He had submitted an outline of his manuscript and several chapters to a few publishers, but had left for Europe before any of them had replied. Now it seemed that one company had tried to reach him, and when he didn't answer a letter, they had telephoned the college.

"Everyone seems to have known I was spending the spring vacation in Europe. Garson said to try me at the house in Arosa. By coincidence one of their editors was in Zürich on business, and he'd like to see me tomorrow before he flies back."

She tried to be as elated over his news as he was, but her feeling of foreboding persisted. "Does Garson know that I'm here with you?"

"How could he? I didn't know I'd be here myself, and certainly I couldn't be sure I'd even find you when I left. No one knows you're here, Iris. I'm sure of that."

She continued to be uneasy, obscurely. "When do you plan to go? Ian, I can't bear the thought of driving all the way down the mountain and then having to come up again."

"You don't have to," he said at once. "You don't have to go with me. It's only a few hours' drive by car to Zürich, and I can leave after breakfast and be back well before dinner. You're not afraid to stay here alone, are you?"

"No," she said slowly. "Why should I be?"

It was while Ian was outside the next morning, clearing the icicles and snow from the car, that Ralph telephoned.

It was not Ralph's voice, and at first she did not recognize him. He said, "Is Dr. Sexton there?"

"I'll call him. Who is this, please?" She thought it might be the editor whom Ian was going to meet. But

258

the voice changed and became Ralph's. She stood stunned, incredulous.

"Iris? It *is* Iris?"

She made herself answer. "Yes. Ralph?"

"Iris, listen. I have to be quick. Can Sexton hear us?"

"He's outside."

"Good. Iris, I don't want him to know I called. Understand? It's imperative. It's a matter of life and death. Your life."

She listened numbly. Outside the window Ian scraped away at the snow on the car, whistling in a brief spell of glittering sunlight.

"I only asked for him to make sure he was there. I would have hung up if he had answered. It was you I came to speak to. I had a hunch you might be together."

"You're here? In Arosa?"

"I'm staying in a pension a little below there. Look, we have to talk, and alone. Does he ever leave you? Or can you get away without making him suspicious?"

"He's leaving for Zürich in a half hour," she said. "He'll be gone for the afternoon."

She was numb with the premonition of disaster. They had found out something. The police knew about Sexton. Some evidence had been uncovered that pointed to him, and soon they would start looking for him. Ralph might even have found it out himself. He had been dissatisfied with the reasons for Aunt Gladys's death, and he had told her even then that he

259

was going to investigate on his own. It had to be important, or he would not have left school to seek her out.

"I'll come there in a half hour. Iris, listen to me. Whatever happens, don't tell Sexton that I'm here, or even that I called. If you want him to know afterwards, that's up to you. But first you have to hear what I've found out."

She put down the telephone. She went to the window and stared at Ian as he finished the windshield, put the brush back into the trunk, stamped up on the porch to clear the snow from his boots. He saw from her expression that something was wrong, but he misinterpreted the cause.

"Iris, it isn't too late for you to change your mind and come along. If you don't want him to see us together you can wait for me in the lobby."

She shook her head. Ralph was coming, and their idyll was ended. Somewhere in the back of her mind she had known it was only that, an idyll, and that it could not last. Sooner or later she would bring calamity down on Ian's head.

He studied her worriedly. "I won't go at all if you mind that much. To hell with Zürich. If they really want the book, they'll wait until we get back to New York to talk about it."

"You should go, Ian. The book is so important to you, and I honestly don't mind staying here."

He was thinking. "Tell you what, I'll leave the car for you, in case you have to get away for any reason. I'll use the Oehrlis' car." The Oehrlis had left a car in the

260

garage, which was why Ian kept theirs outside on the driveway. "Maybe I'd better check it first and make sure it's working."

She waited tensely, afraid Ralph would turn up before he left. He came back into the house, leaving the engine running outside to warm through while he changed into a shirt and tie—to make him seem substantial and dependable, he said, the kind of man who would send in his revisions on time.

"You're sure you won't come along, Iris? Why don't you take the car into Arosa and have lunch at the Valsana? The day won't seem so long."

She nodded. "Maybe I will." From the porch she watched him drive away, saw him turn around to look back at her several times until she was afraid he would run into a tree. And finally she waved him on and went inside. From the doorway she waited until the sound of his motor was absorbed into the silence.

For some minutes she walked around aimlessly, staring at the chalet as if she wanted to impress it forever on her mind. Its raw yellow wood and crude furnishings had long since been mellowed in her eyes by their hours in it. She no longer viewed it as she had at first sight; it had been transformed, like Paris, into a place where they had loved each other.

She thought: I will never be as happy again. She had been happy enough to forget to be afraid, to forget about what had happened at Freebody, to care only that he had made her believe he loved her. It didn't even really matter whether he *did* love her, only that he had made her believe it. She went upstairs and

261

changed the linen on their bed and covered it neatly, as if they would never sleep in it again.

From the balcony she had a clear view down the road. She saw the dark figure of a man approach the house, and her heart clutched painfully. It was Ralph, his cheeks reddened by the cold, his fair hair glinting in the sun, his face remote as if he were intent on inner thoughts. She felt like someone in a besieged city, watching the enemy approach the gates. Only he wasn't the enemy; he had come to save her; he had come now like an avenging angel to strike Ian down. Except that she would be destroyed with him.

She went down to let him in. He kissed and hugged her with profound relief, as if he hadn't really believed he would find her. "Iris, I've been scared as hell about you. It was just the craziest hunch that brought me here."

"Why were you scared about me?" she asked, sitting down because she did not want him to notice the trembling inside her.

"Because of what I found out about him." He sat down opposite her, larger and more handsome than she remembered him. Compared to him, Ian was too dry, too spare, too sharp. *Why don't I feel about you the way I do about Ian? It would be so simple, then.* He said, "I told you I was going to check on a few things, and I did. I learned enough to convince me there's something you must be made to realize about the man before you get in any deeper." He looked up sharply. "You're not married?"

She felt as if she were protecting Ian when she lied. "No."

Relief flashed across his face. "I'm glad. I was afraid I'd find you too late."

"How did you know he was here?" She did not want to listen to his news; she tried to push the moment away.

"I went to Bill Tieman with what I'd found out, and when he heard he told me he didn't know exactly where you were, but that you had bought a ticket to Paris, and he had deposited money in a Paris bank for you. I was planning to go to Paris to look for you when he mentioned that Sexton was in Europe, and he guessed what he was doing. Then I began to think you had planned to meet him in Europe, and so I went to the college to see if they knew where he was, and that's how I heard about this house." He paused. "Iris, the reason you may still be alive is that you're not married yet. He still has nothing to gain by your death."

Uncle Bill knew. She'd had a wild idea that she could plead with Ralph to forget what he knew, to let her be happy a little longer, but now Uncle Bill knew, and he would feel justified in finding them.

"Ralph, I'm in love with him. I don't want to hear anything about Ian. Please don't tell me anything."

"You can't hide from the facts. Iris, don't be a child. I know your being in love is going to make it harder to face, but you're going to be hurt sooner or later, and maybe it will be less painful this way. Iris, Sexton was the prime suspect in his wife's death. They had only circumstantial evidence against him so they had to let him go. But he was in his wife's house the afternoon she died. He admitted that. He said he kept his papers and books there, and he took some that day. Iris, the fire started in the basement. The smoke came up through the ducts and killed his wife while she slept, even before the flames reached the bedroom. Iris, *this is how my mother died.*"

Her voice was as light and dry as a breath. "So do many other people."

"The divorce wasn't final yet, and so Sexton stood to inherit all her property. He would have lost it all if the decree had gone through, and it would have in another few weeks. Iris, face the fact: Two people died providentially for Sexton. I won't bring up Sally Lucas, because I don't know her. But I did hear that there was something going on between them at the time he pretended to be in love with you, and it's possible she may have turned nasty and he had to dispose of her, too. But we won't think about her now. Think of my mother. Think of his wife. Observe the pattern. He got away with it once. Why not again?"

She stared down at her hands. She had remembered to take off her wedding ring and put it in her pocket.

"Iris, for God's sake, are you so infatuated with this murderer that you refuse to see the truth?"

"You haven't proved anything," she said in the same light, dry voice. "It could all be coincidence."

The night Aunt Gladys died he had been downstairs for more than a quarter of an hour. He had said he was in the kitchen looking for something to eat, but he could have heard Aunt Gladys wheezing in her sleep behind the closed door of her sitting room, and entered it, and arranged a burning cigarette on the pillows beside her.

264

"Iris, from the moment he wangled his way into the gatehouse he's had only one purpose—to get you to marry him. He's done away with every obstacle that stood in his way. Me. My mother. Maybe even Sally. Just the way he did away with his wife before their divorce, so that he would still be in her will."

*I came into a little money,* Ian had said. He had bought her a ring of opals with the money he'd received after his wife had burned to death.

"Iris, isn't there any way I can convince you that you're in danger from a man like this? If you marry him, he'll make you believe he loves you. Then one of those years when he's bored, and wants the money with no wife attached, he'll find some way to get rid of you and it will all be his. And he'll work it out so that nothing can be proved, just like the other times. He's intelligent and clever. You know that."

He will make me believe he loves me. He almost has. Could he be thinking while he loves me that this is a house of wood, well away from a town that is half deserted? Could his mind be spinning away: all wood, it would go up in a puff of smoke, over in an instant. Who could reach the chalet on time? Is this what goes on in his thoughts all the while he holds me, and tells me how happy he is? No. Not Ian. She would not believe it of Ian.

She said, "I just want to stay with him."

He stared at her in disbelief. "I won't let you be that stupid!"

"This is the way I want it, Ralph."

"You're asking to be killed! You know what Tieman

or anyone else would say? That I *make* you leave here!"

"Please don't try it, Ralph."

Suddenly and shockingly, his eyes filled with tears. "I've been out of my mind these last months," he said chokingly. "I can't work, I can't think. I walked out on my classes to come here. I can't leave you here with him, Iris. I love you. Even if you don't love me, I can't leave you in the hands of a murderer."

She was aghast at his tears; she had never imagined him capable of them. He was crying because of her. Her own eyes filled. "Ralph, I'm so sorry. What can I say? I don't mean to cause you all this trouble. I wish you would forget about me. Go home, please, and forget about me."

He turned his contorted face from her.

"It's snowing," she said. "Did you walk all the way? Was it far?"

"Not far. A little over a mile and a half."

"You can't walk back. I have the car. I'll drive you back."

"How I get back isn't what's important. But you're asking to be killed, Iris. Asking to be killed."

"You said it yourself. If I'm stupid, it's the way I want it to be."

*I bring disaster to everyone that I know. Not I, but the money. Not only Ian, but Ralph, too. I've wrecked this year for him, maybe wrecked his whole future* How much had he depended on the Freebody name to advance his job chances? How many of those chances would still be open to him? She had laid a shining

266

prospect before him, and then snatched it away. He had lost his mother, his home, his career, everything. "If I knew how to make it up to you, I would," she said.

He didn't answer, walking from her to the window to stare at the thickly falling snow.

"Can I get you some coffee? A drink?"

He shook his head.

She went to him and put her arm through his and pressed his against her. "Please, Ralph, forget about me. Whatever happens to me, it's the way I want it."

He turned around, and the change in his face was marked, the color drained away and his eyes reddened. He muttered, "I may as well go back."

"Let me drive you. Please."

He shrugged.

She ran to get her coat and boots. When she came back he was still standing as he had been when she left him, staring vacantly at the snow.

"You've done everything you can, Ralph. No one could do any more. It's my own decision."

He repeated her words dully. "It's your own decision."

They went outside. She offered to let him drive, but he shook his head, and maybe it was just as well because he seemed too distraught to handle a car. He got in beside her, and they drove down the hill toward Arosa. The skating pond was deserted, and snow was piling up against the stairs of the empty hotels. Across the railroad bridge, and now the steep descent began.

She tried to rouse him from his apathy. "Where are you staying?"

"You wouldn't know it. They only rent a few rooms. It's on this road."

The skin seemed to have stretched too tightly over his face, like gray parchment. "Ralph?" she said anxiously. "Are you sick? Shall I stop the car?"

He turned his gray face toward her. His lips hardly moved as he spoke. "Keep driving," he said.

It was his voice that frightened her most; it seemed to come from an automaton, a flat, dead sound, as if he were catatonic. Her hands felt nerveless on the wheel. She managed to say, "Is it much farther?" He didn't answer.

The road spiraled down relentlessly, always the mountain to one side, always the vast white emptiness paralleling it. Suddenly the car was filled with an icy cold. She turned her head, to see his door swing open wide.

"Ralph! No!"

He was going to jump. He was distraught enough to jump. Too terrified to think, she stepped hard on the brake, and the car went into a slow spin across the road. He fell out and rolled in the snow, while the car slowly revolved and began to slide down the road backward.

"Ralph!"

He was on his feet, sliding and falling as he came around to the driver's seat. He wrenched open her door and reached in. His face was contorted beyond recognition. The wild hope that he was trying to save her died. He struck her hands from the wheel and with a sound from his throat that was curiously like a sob he turned the wheel sharply.

268

The car's front wheels hung over the side of the road for a terrible instant, and then the car flipped in the air like a small toy and fell. She heard the grinding jolts when the doors broke off. Branches blackened the windows as the car careened into trees, sheared its way clear and continued its furious plunge. The wheel pinned her. She felt an agonizing pain as her legs struck metal hard and cracked. Half dislodged, she was face-down in the snow, her body still held behind the wheel, as the car sank to a halt.

The cold snow on her face brought her back to awareness—the cold and the pain. She managed to turn her head. Fluid ran from the car like blood, dark on the snow, and there was a smell of fire. Even as she watched, she saw a small tongue of flame lick the underside of the car. She tried to free herself, but the pain was too much and she blacked out. It seemed to her she heard Ian's voice call her name.

She felt an agony deeper than any thus far, *I don't want to die now! I've been so happy! If I could have had it just a little longer!* And with it the thought: *at least it wasn't Ian. At least my death isn't at his hands.*

# 20

He wasn't happy about leaving her. She was upset; maybe just at the thought of being alone; maybe for some other reason. She's a big girl now; she has to get used to being alone, he told himself. But it didn't make him feel any better. The drop on the open side of the road was even more sheer than it appeared when he had seen it in the dark that night. No wonder she didn't want to make the trip again unnecessarily. And yet, she wasn't the sort of girl to be frightened by a perilous road. There was more to it, as if she were blaming other fears on this, as if a wider anxiety was brought to focus on the road. Or on the chalet; she'd been uneasy when they first came to the chalet, as if its isolation was too much for her. And yet she lived in that grim pile of stones with an aunt who wanted her dead, who would have seen her dead if she'd been brighter and more skillful at murder. She had gotten her fear under control until today, when it had erupted under the stress of his leaving her. Maybe he shouldn't have gone, maybe he should have insisted on her coming along. Hell, he'd be back in six hours. . . .

At a turn in the road a man came out of a small house with a *Zimmer Frei* sign hanging over it, and for no reason that he could think of—and for the first time in a long time—he thought of Ralph. It must have been something in the man's walk that reminded him, because he hadn't caught a glimpse of his face. He craned to look for him, but the man was walking up the road toward Arosa.

He had a feeling she wanted to keep the news of their marriage a secret because of Ralph. She hadn't said so, maybe out of some fine regard for his own feelings—because she didn't want him to guess that she was still concerned about Ralph. He could understand why she didn't want Ralph to know about their marriage. She knew Ralph even better than Ralph knew himself, and she knew that the news would be a stunning blow. What must have sustained Ralph up to now was the hope that she would somehow change her mind and come back to him, and all would be restored, and once more he could look forward to being lord of the manor, lord to Iris. Ralph was too rigid. He couldn't bend, only break, and if he found out about them, he would be destroyed.

It was a wonder he hadn't already tried to do away with Iris. Maybe he hadn't the imagination, or maybe he was too afraid of the risk. He was intelligent, unlike his stepmother, and he could anticipate the consequences. Ralph would never launch an attack unless he was positive he would not fail.

*271*

His uneasiness persisted. Damn it, it was the thought of Ralph that was disturbing him. Ralph didn't know they were married. Ralph thought he was still her only surviving heir. Damn that fellow anyway for making him think of Ralph. And of Iris up there in the chalet alone. It was ridiculous to worry. Ralph had no idea where she was. Even Tieman didn't know. How could he find her? And yet the fellow's walk, the shape of his shoulders . . .

To complicate matters, the snow began to fall with blizzard force. He'd heard of the spring snows, soft and heavy and wet enough to cause slides. What would this be like later when he was driving back? Suppose he couldn't get up the mountain? There was the train. But the train had to climb, too. Suppose it was stalled for several hours and Iris was alone up there all night?

He came down to Chur and filled the tank with gas. The railroad station was not far off. He decided to walk over and find out if the trains were running.

They were. He stood uncertainly in the station for some moments. The trains were running. They were rarely stopped by snow. If he couldn't drive up later he could always take the train. He wandered over to the newsstand, still uncertain, saw a copy of the Paris *Herald* and bought it. He hadn't seen the news from home in a long time. Hell, I can call the fellow in Zürich and tell him I'll see him when we get back, that I can't leave because of the snow. He folded the paper over, and somehow his eye caught a small headline: Man Confesses to Vermont Murder.

He stopped at the entrance of the station to read it.

The caretaker on the Freebody estate in eastern Vermont has confessed to a murder that has baffled the local police in the town of Freebody for several months. Augustus Nearing, age 70, claims to have drowned a young college student of this town, Sally Lucas, because he blamed her for causing the suicide of his grandson five years ago. "She wasn't worth it," Nearing told the police. "She wasn't worth his killing himself over. She was just a tramp." Nearing said he followed the girl for some time and observed her drinking with men in the town, and that one day it was too much for him, and . . .

So it was Nearing. He should have realized that possibility; and maybe he would have, if the aunt's death and Iris's flight hadn't erased everything else from his mind. Maybe he ought to let Iris know—telephone her. No, better not. He'd better be there when she found out so that he could ease it for her. Maybe he would telephone her anyway, find out how she was, if the snow was very bad. . . .

He stepped into a telephone booth and called their number. It rang, but no one answered. He called the number again, but still no answer. He had the operator check, and then he asked her if she was sure she was getting through; perhaps the lines were fouled. But no. There was no problem with the lines.

He walked back to the car and got in, and instead of turning onto the wide new highway to Zürich, he swung around and headed home to Arosa. She probably took the car and went to the Valsana, he told himself. She probably thought she'd be better off there if the snow got too bad. Nothing to worry about, he told himself firmly. She's a big girl, and she can take care of herself. He went up the hill too fast for the snow and the grade and the poor visibility, but his heart was pounding for no known reason. You're acting like a fool, he told himself as the car spun and then righted itself. Crash the car and you won't make it back at all.

He braked suddenly. This was the house he'd seen the man come out of. On a sudden impulse he got out, walked up the shoveled walk to the door and rang.

A woman came to the door.

"I'm looking for a friend. His name is Ralph Forsher. Is he staying here?"

She shook her head, "Nein."

He turned to go. He stopped. "Are you sure? An American—"

"We have an American staying here. His name is Mr. Clark. From Chicago."

"Young?"

"Yes, young. He is not here now. He went out earlier."

"Thanks." He got back into the car and started up the mountain again. Americans walk like Americans. Ralph walked like an American. That was all. A young American would make him think of Ralph. That was all. Damn the snow. He could barely see, even though it was still early afternoon.

A figure was coming out of the snow toward him. He blew the horn sharply. The man stood aside to let him pass.

He turned, and got a look at the man's face. It was Ralph.

274

Ralph looked at him, and his mouth opened, and then closed.

Something funny about the way he looked. "Ralph?" he said. "It's me, Sexton. Is anything wrong?"

"She's dead," Ralph said. "It was an accident. She was driving me back and the car skidded, and I fell out. But she went over. She's dead. You're too late. You'll never marry her now. It was all for nothing."

Ian got out to grab the hulking figure. Ordinarily he was no match for Ralph—but now, somehow he was holding Ralph by the arms and shaking him.

"Where is she? Tell me where she is!"

Ralph gestured. "Down there. But you're too late. She's dead."

He was dragging Ralph into the car, pushing, lifting his legs to shut the door. Ralph was dazed, his body inert. He put his head back against the seat and shut his eyes.

Ian found the tracks of her car, too deep to be entirely obliterated. He jammed on the brake and jumped out. He leaned over the edge. The path of the car was like a fierce scar in the porcelain whiteness of the mountainside, a scar jagged and blackened with oil, doors scattered, headlamps and hubcaps a gruesome litter, like the parts of a human body. The car was too far down to be visible. Only a black smudge could be seen, thin smoke rising from its pyre.

The smoke galvanized him. The car was on fire. It was going to explode. He scrambled down the side, his breath coming in choking gasps. He slid and slipped

*275*

and fell and rolled, hardly aware of the rocky spine of the mountain bruising him.

"Iris!" His voice cracked.

*I'll kill him. I don't care if they put me away for life for it. I'll beat his brains out.* Gasps raked his chest, and there was a film of fury over his eyes.

The flames were already curling under the car. If they reached the gas tank, he would never get her out alive. He slid the last few feet, almost on top of where she lay, half in the car, half in a snowdrift.

Her eyes were open and stayed on him. Her legs were twisted and bleeding behind the steering column. He tried to lift it away, but couldn't. He swore, his eyes blinded by smoke and tears.

"Go away, Ian!" she cried. "The car is going to explode!"

The flames were running in tiny rivulets on the snow. He seized her legs and she screamed. "It's all right, Ian! You can't do anything!"

The heat seared his face as he reached in again. He ripped at her broken legs, and she fainted, fortunately, so he did not have to spare her pain while he pulled frantically until he wrenched her free. The car blew up in a cloud of flame and he rolled over and over in the drifts with her in his arms, blotting out the flaming oil that spattered them in the merciful snow. The flames burned out. He lay beside her, blackened with smoke and grease, fighting for breath.

She opened her eyes. She had to be in terrible pain with her twisted, bleeding legs and her cut and swollen face. But she achieved a smile. "I'm happy," she whispered. He thought she was delirious, except that her voice was so clear, and her eyes, which did not leave his face, were more at peace than he had ever seen them.

The fire brought the police and people from the village, and the ambulance came from Chur. His own car with Ralph in it had vanished. He rode with her to the hospital. The doctors told him that everything broken would mend, everything bruised would heal, and if the cuts left scars, that could be fixed, too.

Bill Tieman flew from Concord when he got Ian's wire, and by that time Iris was well enough to talk. She told Tieman how they got married, and how Ralph came to see them, and how she had skidded over the edge, driving Ralph home. She did not tell Tieman what actually happened, and she made Ian promise not to tell him either. "I want to make it up to him, and this is a way. He won't hurt me again."

Against his inclination, Ian remained silent while Iris told of the miraculous change of mind that made him come back instead of continuing on to Zürich. Maybe she was only trying to convince her uncle that the man she married possessed certain heroic qualities that didn't show on the surface. At any rate, she repeated the story several times, seeming to relish the details of how he'd risked his life to save her. Maybe she just liked to think about it. It seemed to be terribly important to her.

It was Tieman who told her about Nearing's confession. They had kept it from her until she was stronger. Now, coupled with her shock, Ian thought he detected on her face what might be described as relief. She had been more concerned about the cloud of suspicion Sally's death had cast than he had realized. He wondered. . . .

Tieman saved another piece of bad news until the day of his departure.

"I wouldn't tell you this at all now, Iris, except that I don't want it to be a blow to you when you come home. Iris, Miss Coffey is dead."

She turned her face away from them.

"She was failing, you know, and then she had another stroke. She sent me a letter to send on to you, but of course I didn't know where to send it. Here it is."

She read the letter after Tieman left, and then she gave it to Ian to read. It said:

Dear Iris,

You will hate me for what I have to say, but I must say it anyway, because I am old and sick, and when I die I want it to be with a clear conscience.

I let your Aunt Gladys die. I did not kill her. I swear to that. But I did let her die. I wasn't sleeping well anymore, and Dr. Sexton warned me to watch you so that she shouldn't get her hands on you again. So I walked around the house a good part of the night, watching. That's how I smelled the smoke, and went downstairs, and found her. She was unconscious, and maybe she was already dead. But maybe I could have saved her. I didn't. I closed the door and went away.

It was a terrible wrong thing to do, and it has made me

278

sick. But I am not sorry, because she was a selfish, wicked, foolish woman, and she tried to kill you, and she would have tried again. Forgive me if you can, and please don't hate me.

Your Coffey.

He put the letter down. For a while they sat without saying anything. The only sounds were the muted hospital noises outside their door. He felt her eyes resting on him, and after a while he got up and leaned over her and touched her cheek. "It's me. Don't look at me as if you didn't know me."

She said, "I know you, Ian. I just wasn't sure I did, before."

"And what does that mean?"

She said, "It means, I know you love me."

"Didn't you know that?" He considered, then said soberly, "Well, maybe I didn't know how much, myself, before."

He sensed there was more that might be said, but no more was necessary.